every crawling, putrid thing

david busboom

JOURNALSTONE
YOUR LINK TO ARTIST TALENT

This is a work of fiction. All of the characters, names, incidents, organizations, and dialogue in this novel are either the products of the author's imagination or are used fictitiously.

The views expressed in this work are solely those of the authors and do not necessarily reflect the views of the publisher, and the publisher hereby disclaims any responsibility for them.

ISBN: 978-1-68510-039-1 (sc)
ISBN: 978-1-68510-040-7 (ebook)
Library of Congress Control Number:

First printing edition: April 8, 2022
Printed by JournalStone Publishing in the United States of America.
Cover Design: Don Noble
Edited by Sean Leonard
Proofreading and Cover/Interior Layout: Scarlett R. Algee

JournalStone Publishing
3205 Sassafras Trail
Carbondale, Illinois 62901

JournalStone books may be ordered through booksellers or by contacting:
JournalStone | www.journalstone.com

table of contents

For Dad, fire-breathing DJ and master shipbuilder of my childhood

And for Mom, who never stopped reading with me

every crawling, putrid thing

can't stop here

I'M DOING SIXTY somewhere around Atwood on the edge of the county, listening to a Stephen King story on tape. It's after midnight and the moon hovers bright and full in the sky, racing me home. In the passenger's seat lies a VHS copy of *One Million B.C.* that's older than I am, my most recent treasure from the Record Swap store in Champaign. On the garish cardboard cover, a spear-wielding Victor Mature protects Carol Landis from a giant iguana under the sensational tagline: SEE PREHISTORIC CAVEMEN BATTLE SAVAGE MONSTERS AT THE DAWN OF TIME! Sarah didn't like the movie as I hoped she would; she thinks "slurpasaur" effects constitute animal abuse. She's right, of course, but I still find the optically enlarged reptiles somehow charming.

She wants us to take a dance class together next semester, when we'll both move out of our parents' houses and transfer from community college to a proper university. Slow-dancing with her in an empty room has always been enough for me. She's hinted that she'd like us to share an apartment as well, but though I love her I'm not convinced we're ready for that after only a year and a half of dating. When I tell her these things, she acts melancholy and implies that I'm a coward, not willing to take a risk.

"Live a little," she says.

Suddenly there's a terrible roar and the sky's full of rain and huge bats, swooping and diving around the car. Amid the storm of furry bodies, an enormous winged thing hits the windshield with a jarring *crack*, leaving a forked lightning-bolt across the glass. My breath catches in my throat and a noise comes out that's not quite a scream. I smash the brake pedal to the floor and aim the old white Buick toward the shoulder, my trembling hands barely managing the wheel.

It's quiet again, except for the messy drumroll of rain. I stare up at the clouds through the broken windshield and turn on the wipers, let out a long, quivering sigh. The bats are still there, their bodies flashing in my headlights. The smallest of them must be as big as an eagle, the biggest… Well, I'm not sure. I think I see a wingtip like a great shark's fin, brushing my window. I close my eyes.

Still have at least fifteen miles to go. I consider turning around, going back to Atwood, back to Sarah, but I'm more than halfway home. In any case I can't stop here like this. The bats might begin landing on the car, maybe try to break in. There are so many—I can only see a dozen or so at a time in my headlights, but there must be hundreds or even thousands of them. I'll have to ride them out.

The bats themselves are silent or nearly so; I can't hear any screeching from inside the car. That brief but ear-blasting roar came from my radio, like a burst of unbelievably bad static with the volume turned way up—except the volume wasn't. The Stephen King tape was playing at no more than half volume, and presently I notice that it's stopped playing altogether. I pull carefully back onto the now-slick road, eject the tape and push it back in, make sure the volume is, in fact, turned low. But instead of Yeardley Smith's Lisa Simpson voice backed by ominous music, my ears are assaulted by another piercing wail, this one more high-pitched. It begins as an almost metallic shriek, and then becomes something else, something wild.

Something like the sound of many, many bats.

With a little gasp, I eject the tape and throw it into the passenger's seat. I expect to hear classical music on 90.9 WILL, but there's nothing. After a minute I touch the preset buttons, tuning the radio to my other favorite stations, but they're silent as well. I need music, talk, something to keep me calm. Driving slow, letting the bats fly around me rather than risk more smashing into my windshield like enormous moths, I pop in a Moody Blues tape that's also sitting in the passenger's seat. I hear the first ten seconds or so of "Gemini Dream" before the music distorts into that same merciless cry. It seems my only options are silence or that awful bat noise. I opt for silence.

I drive on that way for a while, never going more than twenty miles an hour, like someone driving through a blizzard. The bats are endless. I think of Sarah, probably asleep by now. How she said once that she's seen things on the road at night, driving home from my place in Champaign. Weird trees, huge shadows sliding across the road from out of the barren cornfields. She dismissed them all as tricks of the eye.

My windshield and windows begin to fog up, as they do in heavy rain or cold weather. This is not a warm night, certainly wet enough, and the fog comes quick and thick on my windows; much too quick. I turn on the defogger, but it does nothing to clear the mist from my windshield, only slowing the steady increase in opacity. In minutes I can barely see where I'm going, and I reduce my speed even further.

My ears pop, as though my elevation has abruptly changed. At once the rain lightens from a downpour to a drizzle, the fog recedes from my windows, and I notice that even the bats are thinning a bit. I see what look like bizarre trees, dotting the landscape on both sides of the road.

My heart thuds in my chest, my stomach drops into my groin. I see gigantic shapes silhouetted against the moonlit sky, just discernible through the bat-cloud. I make out only three, two on my right and one on my left, but there must be more of them beyond my range of vision. They're bigger than hippos, with huge heads and humped backs lined with long spines, but I can make out no other details in the bat-cluttered darkness.

I try to turn my attention back to the road itself. Its monotony comforts me, feels like a good sign. It's the only familiar thing in a now totally unfamiliar environment, and I'm certain that wherever I am, surely no longer in Piatt or Douglas or even Champaign County, the road will lead me out. If I just follow it, focus on it, keep going, I'll be okay, even if it takes hours to reach the next town.

My eyes keep darting back to the large moving things that, I'm sure, are getting closer. If one of them attacks, can I outrun it? I'm sure I can, though doing so will mean running into perhaps hundreds of bats and probably wrecking the car, only for the whatever-it-is to catch up and do whatever-it-wants anyway.

As if on cue, my headlights catch a pair of huge round eyes some distance in front of me. I hit the brakes so hard the cassette tapes in the passenger's seat slide onto the floor, but the thing has already materialized out of the darkness.

It's tall as a man at the shoulder and at least twenty feet long, advancing slowly on four doglike legs with clawed feet that aren't quite paws. Its body is covered with gray-green scales. Its massive head resembles that of a goanna, albeit a nightmarishly exaggerated one, with bulging opaque eyes and serrated, blade-like teeth protruding from its jaws. A rhinoceros-like horn juts from its nose, and a single row of sharp spines lines its humped back, ending at the base of a long tail. Except for its doglike gait, the creature reminds me all too much of Victor Mature's iguana nemesis.

It stops and stares at me a moment, then continues, snapping at the bats. They part before it, swooping around and above as it stalks closer on its weird dog legs. It's only a yard or so from my car now. I glance in the rearview, preparing to flee in reverse, and see another pair of eyes, red this time, reflecting my brake lights.

I'm surrounded.

My hands are shaking. My whole body is shaking. I think I may be sick.

The monster in front of me slows to a stop and lowers its head in an almost regal bow. Its eyes, flashing in my relentless headlights, meet mine on the way down. Those are malevolent eyes, wild and empty but also cruel. They gleam with a dead, animal intelligence, a sort of stupid cunning. How did Warren Zevon put it?

Reptile wisdom.

I put the car back in drive and try to weave around the beast, but it takes up almost the entire road. It moves its head to block me, and its horn scrapes across the Buick's front grille and bumper and punches out my right headlight. Abruptly it is less distinct, partially rejoined with the darkness that birthed it. But it's still there, big and solid as ever. I try again to skirt along the edge of the road, feeling my left front tire dip a little toward the ditch. The lizard-thing nudges its head to the right and the Buick's front is jerked along with it. I scream, a terrified child on a too-intense carnival ride. It's seized the right front tire in its jaws. It tugs at the rubber, snapping its head back like a crocodile trying to rip flesh from a corpse or a dog trying to cheat at tug-of-war. I throw the car in reverse and spin my wheels, but the lizard-thing's grip is like a vice. It sets its feet and holds on as the rear tires whine and throw up smoke.

The Buick jolts from an impact behind me and I bounce in my seat. The rearview shows me that the second monster has planted a clawed forepaw on the trunk and is pressing down, leaning on the car as if to hold it there. The metal groans in protest, the creature's weight causing it to pucker around the edges of that strange foot. Will it climb the car? Its head is no longer visible in my brake lights, only its humped shoulder and part of its broad flank.

The tires continue to throw up smoke, but the car doesn't budge. My pulse races and I feel hot tears behind my eyes. My seatbelt feels tight, constricting. I unbuckle it. My wrist brushes my thigh and hip, and I feel a rectangular bulge in my jeans pocket.

My phone.

Of course! I remove it with a triumphant cry and dial the first number that comes to mind: Sarah, whom I kissed goodnight no more than thirty minutes ago after sharing a pizza in her living room and struggling to hook her parents' ancient VCR up to their big new TV. I want to tell her how much I'd love for us to share a dance class, an apartment, even a life. My fingers take forever to find her name and hit the CALL button.

It doesn't matter. My phone refuses to complete the call. A short message glares up at me in tiny white block letters: NO SERVICE.

With a sob I chuck my phone across the passenger seat. It strikes the window with a loud, hard *thump* and bounces onto the floor. The Buick lurches from behind and I hear the rearward lizard-thing's snout tapping on the roof of the car.

There is a harsh tug beneath me. The lizard-thing has withdrawn from the no doubt-mangled front wheel and a torn half-circle of rubber hangs from its bottom jaw, impaled on teeth like Buck knives. It opens its jaws again and this time clamps down on the front of the car itself, the round Buick hood ornament vanishing beneath a row of those cruel teeth. The metal crumples like tin, and for an eye-blink moment fascination overcomes fear as I wonder how much biting power must reside in those jaws. A few of the bats circle closer.

The Buick rocks metal squeals and groans. The rearward lizard-thing is climbing up. The roof sags and the back windows shatter. I expect to be assaulted by bat noise, but the flying things are as quiet as they were behind glass. I hear a low, quivering moan; mine, though I don't feel it. The car is a deathtrap. I have to get out.

But I need a weapon, anything to keep the monsters at bay. I reach behind the seat. Carpet, bits of broken glass—a shaft of cold metal. I close my fingers around it. My ice scraper: four feet of hollow steel ending with a six-inch blade. I bring the tool forward and manage a small laugh in spite of myself. The heavy-duty scraper has been there for months, untouched since the spring thaw. The blade is sharp, the handle long and sturdy.

Thus armed, I stab the unlock button with my index finger, hear a gratifying *ch-chunk*, and throw open the door with a yell. The night air is damp and chilly. I'm exposed, unprotected—but the Buick's doomed. I throw myself feet-first onto the pavement and my momentum carries me off the road, into the darkness. I stumble into the ditch, much deeper than I thought, and bump hands-first into a twisted hulk of metal.

A car, wrecked in the ditch by the same monsters that tear and prod at the old Buick fifteen feet behind me. I turn around just in time to see a gaping maw, a mess of serrated teeth and forked tongue and rank saliva, bearing down on me.

I scream and swing the ice scraper like a madman, striking the roof of the lizard-thing's mouth. It ducks back with incredible speed, but doesn't flee. It stalks forward slowly, its mouth opening again to produce a rasping, guttural hiss that's almost a roar. I make out a dark gash where the blade hit, and feel a rush of brutal satisfaction.

I am Victor Mature against the optically enlarged iguana—

No, I am Tumak of the Rock Tribe, facing some monstrous relation of the dinosaurs—

It rushes me again.
I swing my spear.

the 800-pound gorilla in the room

"DOUG, I WISH you'd listen to yourself."

Amanda sat on the living room floor, rocking back and forth on her bottom and cooing to herself, while Mom and Dad argued in the kitchen. Albert stretched out on the couch and sipped at his tall glass of ice-cold milk, watching Amanda and wishing he could be out riding his bike instead.

"What? What's wrong with what I just said?"

It was too hot to ride bikes anyway, but Albert wanted—*needed*—to pop a wheelie, a *big* wheelie, preferably in front of a crowd, if for no other reason than to show that smug sixth-grader Timmy Vivant that he could.

"Oh, I don't know, that you *regret* it?"

Timmy had spit on him at lunch the other day, hocked a big ol' loogy right on the back of Albert's head. It must've been easy, Timmy being so tall and all. He'd whipped around only to be face-to-chest with the older boy, whose white-and-blue striped polo somehow looked both too big and too small. He'd had to crane his neck to meet the ginger's stupid snaggle-toothed grin.

"Well, what if I do?"

Albert had wanted to bag Timmy right in the balls, bag him *good*, so he'd drop to his knees right there in the lunch line. Then maybe Albert could spit on *his* head...

But he hadn't. Instead he'd wiped the loogy away with a napkin and moved on to the corner table to sit with his fellow fifth-grade nerds. He'd shot Timmy a nice hot glare, the kind of look Dad said burned holes in people, but it hadn't been very satisfying.

"I just can't believe that. After all we went through, after all this time. What, do you want to call the lab and give her back?"

Albert smiled at the thought of burning holes in Timmy Vivant and sipped at his milk. He'd been upset when Mom had made them all switch to one-percent for Dad's heart, but he'd gotten used to the difference.

"What the hell would I want to do that for?"

Little Amanda was sitting on the floor, playing with her toes now. Albert watched her, his baby sister in her little dark curls and red ladybug dress, and sipped his milk. She almost seemed to shimmer in the sunlight that streamed in through the window.

"You know damn well that's *just* what you want!"

Albert glanced back over the top of the couch. Mom was standing in the middle of the kitchen, by the stove, waving her arms near her sides as she talked. The from-scratch mac n' cheese and fresh garden peas she'd been making were all but forgotten. Supper would be late again.

"It's just that it's different now than it was."

Albert remembered the first time he'd seen Amanda as The Ape. It seemed forever ago now. A mouse had somehow gotten into the living room while they were watching Amanda's favorite movie, *Mighty Joe Young*—one of Dad's creaky old black-and-whites; Albert knew there was a more recent color version, and remembered wondering why they weren't watching that one instead. Amanda had stood up in terror when the mouse ran across her foot, and suddenly she was seven feet tall and covered in thick black hair, with a nine-foot arm span, two-inch canines, and dark brown eyes. She stayed that way for a while, pacing to and from the kitchen on her knuckles like a nervous animal, even after Dad had caught the mouse and taken it outside. Albert had cried, his own terror locking him to the couch even after she'd returned to the living room and turned back into a girl, but he didn't like to think about that part.

Mom and Dad had a lot of explaining to do that night.

"Oh, all right, so let's send her away. Everything would be fine, right?"

Between mumbled words of comfort and apology, they'd told Albert that Amanda was a mutant, being hurt by bad people Mom used to work for. Mom and Dad had rescued Amanda, *adopted* her, just like they'd told him when he'd first met her there, in the living room, some weeks before. So, they hadn't *really* lied—but it was a secret. Because if anyone found out they had her, Amanda might be taken away from them, taken back to the bad people who'd been hurting her. Keeping her here, keeping her a secret, was the right thing to do.

Dad's open palm came down hard on the countertop.

"Jesus, Margaret, you know I don't want anything to happen to her."

That was during third grade. Amanda had been a toddler, and she'd barely changed since, except to be The Ape every once in a while. Albert had grown to like The Ape, after a fashion, but there was something horrible about it all the same. Albert hadn't been able to play in the living room since the day of the mouse. It just wasn't the same anymore, pretending to be a monster between the couches. Not with a *real* monster sitting between them.

"Oh, fine, Doug." Mom had that sarcastic tone she knew Dad hated. Albert cringed, knowing this meant the fight was far from over. "Fine. I'm sure some other family would be happy to take her in, make her safe."

They kept at it, as they had more and more in recent years. They would probably get Divorced, Albert thought, just like Timmy Vivant's parents, if it wasn't for Amanda. As Timmy had proven, a mere son wasn't enough to hold a failing marriage together.

When Albert turned back to Amanda, she was The Ape.

She was very near, her too-human eyes pleading. One gigantic, ink-black finger pointed at his glass of milk. Albert shook his head violently no. She'd been getting in his face like this a lot in recent months, always mooching his snacks and taking sips from his juice. More often than not she was The Ape when she did it, like she knew that form made it harder for him to refuse her, harder to ignore her.

"Oh, don't be like that, Margaret. Don't you *'fine'* me. Just don't. This is *real*."

Amanda, The Ape, kept pointing at Albert's glass, inching her huge body even closer to the couch. She screwed her protruding mouth into a gorilla's approximation of a puppy-dog expression.

"*No*," Albert said, holding the glass closer to his chest.

"Well, *excuse me!* You think I don't know we're talking about our *children?*"

Amanda stopped pointing, reached for the glass. Even on her knuckles, she towered over Albert on the couch. The pleading had gone out of her eyes.

Albert swatted her hand away.

"I said *no*," he snapped. "It's *mine*. You'll just barf it up on the carpet anyway."

He'd never snapped at her like that before. But her looming so close, demanding what was by every right *his*, reminded him of Timmy Vivant grinning down at him. It made him mad. He took a long gulp of milk, giving The Ape his best burning-holes-in-you glare.

Amanda stared at him, her eyes brightening. A deep grunt issued from somewhere in her throat, too low for Mom and Dad to hear.

"We only have one child, Margar—"

She reached for the glass again, faster this time. Faster than Albert could evade or intercept. He had an eyeblink's moment to realize that maybe he wasn't safe, maybe he should've been more careful, before the giant hand closed around his, squeezing it until the glass broke, crushing it until the shards sliced his flesh and the bones cracked.

Albert screamed.

The house was silent for a heartbeat as he sucked in a breath and Mom and Dad turned to look, their fight interrupted. Then he was screaming again, and so were they. Amanda was still holding his hand, still squeezing it, and now she was hooting loudly.

For Albert, the entire house seemed to fade away. The pain was unbearable. Blood and milk welled out between The Ape's fingers, dripping down onto Albert's lap and forming little pink puddles in the folds of his jeans before soaking in. He shut his eyes to keep from vomiting.

"Just let go now, honey!" he heard Mom shriek. He wondered if she was urging him to faint, or to die. Then she clarified her addressee: "*Amanda!* Let go, Amanda! *Let go, LET GO OF HIM!*"

Albert felt The Ape's grip tighten, felt the bones grind together, felt the shards cut deeper.

He felt her start to tug at his arm.

Oh my God she's going to rip off my arm, rip it right out of the socket just like the guy did to the monster in that story Dad read—

He couldn't scream anymore, but his face was wet with tears. Mom wasn't screaming anymore either, but she was mumbling quietly, a mile a minute. Alternating between begging God to intervene with promises of devotion and begging Amanda to let go with promises of candy. He couldn't hear Dad's voice at all.

Then Amanda—The Ape—screamed, *roared*—

—and let go.

Albert opened his eyes, careful to look anywhere but at the mangled ruin of his hand. Amanda was pawing at a white tuft that looked like the birdies they used for badminton in gym class. It stuck out of her chest like a conical flower. The Ape backed away from the couch, stumbled, and collapsed in a twitching black heap.

Albert saw Dad enter the living room, holding a skinny green gun. Then he glimpsed his hand, and knew no more.

***

He came to still lying on the couch, feeling groggy. His hand hurt a lot, but not as bad as before. Risking a look, he saw it was bandaged, with each finger set in a metal-and-plastic splint and the whole thing arranged in a padded sling across his chest.

Albert felt like some kind of crippled cyborg. It might've been almost cool if it didn't still hurt so much, and if his assailant wasn't still in the room.

The Ape was asleep on the floor, belly-up. He wondered if she would be sorry when she woke up, and realized he didn't even care. He *hated* Amanda, hated her even more than Timmy Vivant.

Mom and Dad were sitting on the other couch, talking in harsh whispers. They didn't seem to notice that he was awake.

"We should've taken him to the hospital, Margaret."

"And told them what?"

The house was dark, except for the soft glow from a solitary lamp and the brighter light from the kitchen. It was late. Albert's stomach growled inaudibly, and he realized they'd never eaten dinner.

"We could've staged a break-in, told them we don't know where the ape came from…"

"'*The ape*'? Is that all she is to you now?"

Dad had taken the form of a little boy. Himself, at about Albert's age, complete with a t-shirt advertising some long-forgotten cartoon from the 1990s. The skinny green gun looked like a comically large toy in his hand.

He looks just like me.

"Margaret, let's cut the bullshit." Hearing little-boy Dad cuss was even funnier than seeing him with the gun, but Albert couldn't laugh. This was all too real. "Things have changed. It just won't be possible to keep her here anymore. She won't obey."

"I can't believe you *shot* her."

"It was just a damn tranquilizer, and I didn't have a choice! She attacked our *son*."

"And *I* went to *five* different pharmacies to get the supplies we needed—"

"Right! You *had* to do that just to avoid suspicion, when a *real* doctor could've helped him better and fast—"

"*Christ*, Doug, you said yourself he's going to be okay! And turn that thing off, I can't take you seriously looking like that."

"Sorry, I didn't mean to. You know how sensitive it can be."

Dad picked up a tiny white rectangle from the little end table—the living room remote—and pointed it at the ceiling, pressing a button. The little boy fizzled and faded away, leaving grown-up Dad in his place.

"Why would Amanda hurt Albert?" Mom started to cry. "My God, she *likes* Albert!"

"She's been mature for a while. Maybe captivity is making her aggressive."

"She's not in *captivity*. We *rescued* her from 'captivity.'"

"You know what I mean. She's cooped up, when all she probably wants is to run around in the woods, like we used to let her before the developments started popping up. Now she doesn't even get fresh air."

Albert looked over at The Ape, still lying on the floor. Mom or Dad had removed the empty dart, but one giant hand was still cupped over the massive chest. It rose and fell with slow, steady rhythm.

"How long until she wakes up?"

"Shouldn't be much longer."

"You going to shoot her again?"

Dad started to say something, hesitated.

"Only if I have to," he said at last.

"Oh, Doug, what are we going to *do?*"

"I don't know. She's too heavy to move on our own, if she won't go to her room…"

Her room was Dad's workshop, once upon a time. Just off the living room. It was bigger than Albert's, upstairs.

"She will," Mom said. "I'm *sure* she will. What about Al?"

"He can stay home from school for a few days, but he's got to go back sometime. His hand will be messed up. People will ask about it."

Albert hadn't considered that. He wondered what Timmy Vivant would say when he went back to school with a crooked hand.

I'll bag him good if he so much as snickers.

He only wished he could do the same to The Ape. Instead, he'd have to settle for burning holes in her from a distance.

"We'll have to come up with something, I guess."

"Like what?"

"Oh, I don't know, Doug. Maybe…maybe Al slammed his hand in the car door."

"Himself? By accident?"

"Of course. What else could it be but an accident? He slammed his hand in the car door."

"You almost sound like you believe it already yourself."

"We'll all have to believe it, to make it work. And just what's that supposed to mean, anyway?"

"Nothing. But how could he even do that to himself? By accident?"

"Okay, well, maybe *you* did it."

Dad shot her a glare, burning holes better than Albert ever could.

"If either of us did this, it was you."

Mom stared back at him, opened her mouth as if to pursue the matter, and then seemed to think better of it. Dad sighed. "She'll be awake soon," he said.

The three of them watched the sleeping gorilla on the living room floor, and waited.

from the dusty mesa

WHEN I WAS six, I met a hoodoo man.

This was in the summer of 1958; my family was on vacation in Mississippi and we were exploring Vicksburg. While my parents window-shopped, I stalked around their legs and watched the people on the sidewalk. That's when I saw him at the end of the block.

He was an old black man in an antique wooden wheelchair, with wiry legs no thicker than my own six-year-old limbs, and hard-looking arms wide as my torso, I guess from rolling himself around everywhere. He was facing the street, watching the cars go by, I thought, but when I took a step toward him, he turned his head and looked at me like he'd known I was there the whole time. His scalp was covered in patches of thick, tight curls that were more black than gray, and his eyes smiled even though his mouth did not. One eye—the left—looked a little milky. The other was bright as glass.

I went over to him then, told him hello in my meek six-year-old voice. I said my name was Tommy and he said his name was Moses and I saw his teeth. He had a soft, deep voice. I said did he mean Moses like from the Bible and he said yessuh and I said I never read the Bible but my mommy and daddy talked about it. He pointed a bony claw at my parents and said was that my mommy and daddy and I said yes and he said his mommy and daddy were slaves before he was born. I said what were they after he was born and he said his daddy was a corpse and his mommy was a magic woman and I said what's a magic woman and he got real serious and said a vessel of the Masked Prophet.

"Anythin' you do is the plan of the Masked Prophet, understand," he explained. "The Pallid One. He has somethin' to do with everythin' you do, if it's good or bad, He has somethin' to do with it. Just what's for you, you'll get it."

"That sounds like God," I said.

"He's a little like God, not quite as powerful, but a little more practical, maybe." He paused thoughtfully, searching for a way to explain. "Whenever I'm afraid of goin' to Hell I read the Bible and pray to God. Whenever I'm afraid of someone doin' me harm in this world I turn to the Masked Prophet. He came from way back yonder the time the Bible's Moses lived, before the Bible was written or the church found. But you won't find Him in there."

"Why not?"

He looked into my eyes, his right eye sharp. "Not sure myself, but I 'spect it's 'cause the Bible says we was made in God's image. The Masked Prophet ain't that way. He says we more like fleas on a rat—but He still looks after us who know Him." He added this last as though trying to be comforting; whether to me or himself, I don't know.

"What does he look like?"

He frowned. "He's big and thin, with long pale robes. Terrible to look on; never seen His face though, on account of that mask."

After that my parents noticed where I was and with whom I was talking and they pulled me away, apologizing to the old cripple for letting their child bother him but really thinking it was Moses who'd bothered me. They marched me swiftly away, warned me never to approach strangers— especially strangers like *that*—and we finished our vacation and went home to Chicago without mentioning it again.

Over the years I forgot all about the hoodoo man and his strange words. I started reading true crime stories, smoking cigars, drinking whisky, chasing freckled girls and homicidal maniacs. I moved to Texas. I grew a mustache. I got married, shot at, divorced. I barely remembered that I'd ever even been to Mississippi.

Now, crouching in the South Texas desert outside Raptor Mesa, Beretta in hand and almost thirteen years eligible for retirement, I have Moses on my mind.

***

In quiet dusk, under the swollen moon, I am reborn. The Pallid One is in the wind, in the rocks, and I walk with Him among the blooming *opuntia*. His eyes watch me from every direction, but they are not like the eyes of the old men at the hospital; no lust in His gaze, only pure love and warmth. I wonder if He will let me see Him tonight. He let me see Him once before, after the *adicto*, but He wouldn't unmask for me. He said I must do more if I want to see His face. I do.

Carmelita is meeting me out here tonight. She doesn't know He is with me.

***

The first body was found toward the end of May, not even three weeks ago. Naked, middle-aged Caucasian male, clothes scattered about in a twenty-foot radius, bones exposed in places where scavenging animals had torn away the flesh, eyes and genitals eaten away, flies and yellow maggots crawling in the wounds. Ugly and grim, but little I hadn't seen before in four decades of law enforcement. No obvious cause of death, but in the corpse's mouth was a playing card, the King of Clubs, on the back of which were two lines neatly typed:

> When the gibbous moon and black stars rise,
> The Pallid One has a thousand eyes.

For the first time in over fifty years I remembered Moses in Vicksburg. I ran the capitalized phrase through every search engine and database available, but found nothing useful—only brief, dated references as vague as the message on the card. Forensic analysis indicated that the note was typed on a Smith Corona manual typewriter, and yielded no usable fingerprints.

For kicks, I searched for records of men named Moses living in Vicksburg during the late fifties and found only a bare-bones 1959 obituary for a Moses Wells, aged seventy-eight; a taxidermist, no family, never married. No photograph.

Expired driver's license in the corpse's discarded shorts identified it as Murray Browne, a local junkie who hadn't been seen for about two weeks and had probably only been missed by his dealer. Next of kin was a cousin two states away who claimed not to have spoken to Browne in almost fifteen years and wanted nothing to do with him now.

Autopsy revealed a small puncture wound in Browne's neck, and that the cause of death was a probable morphine overdose. It also revealed that, though all of the bite wounds were inflicted postmortem, the oldest teeth marks appeared to be human.

A search of Browne's home—a rundown three-room trailer with dim furniture and lighting—yielded the typewriter: a pale blue model from the seventies. And next to the machine, a full deck of playing cards, minus the kings. There was a small radio and several books, but no television, computer, or phone—though there was no sign of a struggle and little indication that such items had ever been there. I doubted a robbery. There were also various pieces of drug paraphernalia (including syringes and needles, but none that matched the puncture wound), a small bag of heroin, a loaded Smith & Wesson .38 Special revolver, and scattered sheets of paper containing mediocre poetry occasionally referring to a "Maria" and, more often, a "Carmelita" (presumably written by Browne), but no morphine and no further references to "the Pallid One." Only prints in the place were Browne's.

"Carmelita" was the popular moniker of Carmen Jimenez, a stripper at the Dragon's Lair near the edge of town. I'd seen her there more than a few times myself; petite Latina in her early thirties, very pretty face, black hair trimmed short like a little boy's and gelled into spikes up front. The few locals who recalled seeing Browne two weeks prior said he'd been at the Lair, so when I went there to ask around I figured Jimenez was a good place to start. She said he'd been there often in the past few months, and that she was his favorite for lap dances, when he could afford them. I asked her if they had any relationship outside the Lair, and she said not to tell anybody but she didn't swing that way if I knew what she meant. I did.

"When was the last time you saw Mr. Browne?"

"Must be a little over two weeks ago. He came in like normal, had a few drinks, bought a dance from me and tried to flirt, *como siempre*. Poor Murray."

"Did he talk about anything unusual? Any special problems he was having? Strange people he'd met?"

"No, just flirted." She giggled sadly. "Joked about pawning his TV so he could keep seeing me."

"Anything else happen?"

"No, he left right after the dance."

"Was he alone?"

Jimenez nodded. "Yes. He was always solo."

"Okay. Do you know anyone named Maria? The name came up in some—uh—papers we found at Mr. Browne's home."

She looked surprised. "Only two: Maria Peraza and Maria Vasquez. Peraza works here, but I don't think Murray ever bought a dance from her. She didn't like him anyway."

"Is she here tonight?"

"No, she's off tonight. But she'll be in tomorrow."

"What about Vasquez?"

"She's a nurse at Borderland. Took care of my mama last year before she passed, we became friends." She blushed. "Not very chatty though. Think she got some issues herself."

"Did she know Mr. Browne?"

"No idea. Murray was a little crazy, I guess, but I don't know if he was ever in the ward."

"All right, one last thing. Does the phrase, 'the Pallid One,' mean anything to you?"

She looked puzzled. "No, should it?"

Now it was my turn to shake my head. "No, probably not. Thanks for your time, Miss Jimenez."

She smiled, and it put lights in her green eyes. "*Carmelita. Ya lo sabes,* Tom."

I smiled back. "*No cuando es un asunto oficial,* I don't."

"*Muy bien,*" she smirked. "*Detective Wilson.*"

I made a circuit of the Lair, interviewed the other patrons and dancers present, but learned nothing new. I called the Borderlands House psych ward and learned that Browne had briefly checked himself in almost a year ago, stayed one week, and checked himself out. Couldn't tell me why, but said he'd been well-behaved and cooperative. When I asked to speak to Maria Vasquez, the woman on the phone said she was out sick and was expected back in a day or two. Said Vasquez was quiet, but good with patients. Said there'd been a minor incident back in March with a couple of the lecherous older men in the ward, but it had been handled. She couldn't recall Vasquez having any contact with Browne during his stay.

I looked Vasquez up: another Latina about Jimenez's age, maybe a little older, and almost as pretty, with dark hair that hung past her shoulders; a US citizen for nearly twenty years, no criminal record. I doubted her involvement or usefulness.

I returned to the Lair the following night and interviewed Peraza, a twenty-something with dark eyes and large breasts. She was disgusted at the mention of Browne, not surprised or upset by his passing, and tight-lipped. Said she was working during Browne's approximate time of death, which I confirmed with the manager on my way out. I looked her up and found a previous arrest for drug possession, when she was a teenager. Paid a fine, spent six months in jail, and had been working at the Lair since she turned eighteen. Born and raised in Raptor Mesa. I doubted her involvement too, but she'd seen Browne on a fairly regular basis in the months before his murder, and her reticence made me suspicious. I decided to try and get a warrant to search her home. You never know what might prove useful in a case like this—or what weird things people are into.

***

The silver moon and the summer air help Him guide my hands. We are both naked, and I kill her like I did the *adicto*: a quick sting in the throat while we kiss. Her arms fall away from me and she stumbles backward, quivering and gasping shallowly like a fish. She looks at me before she loses balance and I see confusion in her face. I want to take it back, but He caresses me and breathes in my ear, and I know it is what He wants.

She lands on her side, on top of an *opuntia* tangle, and rolls face-down in the sand; the cactus thorns stick in her skin, turning her into a mutant hybrid of some spiny creature. The gasping stops. I kneel over her and touch her trembling hand, wanting to cry but knowing He would not approve. Then she is still.

He appears then, a pale shadow in the moonlight, and tells me to finish my work. I don't want to, but I know He'll never unmask for me otherwise. I must make Him happy. I must see His face.

***

Last night Carmen Jimenez never showed up for work. She was reported missing by a friend this morning. Nobody had seen or heard from her since night before last, and nobody knew where she'd gone.

I'm kneeling over her corpse now, less than half a mile from where Browne was found. In the boiling Texas sun, the flies are imperturbable. She's naked, lying on her back, full of prickly pear spines on one side, small puncture wound in the other side of her neck, clothes in a loose pile just a few yards away. When I found her there were a few black vultures gathered around. I scared them off with a couple of shots from my Beretta, but they'd already taken the softest pieces of her.

There are bites missing from her torso and limbs, though, that aren't the vultures' work. Ragged crescents and ovals made by a smallish mouth, spaced far apart on her body. Such deliberate placement was not detectable on the nearly half-eaten Browne. I touch Carmelita's skin and my fingers come away bloody. There's a throbbing pressure in my head and a tightness in my chest and I think I may be sick, or cry, or both.

Delicately, gripping its edges with thumb and blood-tipped forefinger, I pull the playing card from between her teeth: the King of Hearts. On the back another typed couplet:

Though songs are sung and tears are shed,
The Pallid One is never dead.

"Goddamn it," I sigh.

The blood is pounding in my ears. I'm thinking of Moses when a shadow falls over me. Before I can turn the pain comes, sharp and quick, in my back. It's gone as quickly as it arrives and now I feel tired and much too warm on this already hot day. I pitch forward and heave myself to one side to avoid landing on Jimenez. I'm nauseous and dizzy, on my back in the blood-speckled sand. I can barely hold my head up, can barely breathe. My head is pounding. Maria Vasquez stands over me, wearing frayed jeans and a stained John Lennon t-shirt, syringe held up in one latex-gloved hand. Behind her a tall, thin figure looms, nearly twice as high as the man-sized creosote bushes. It wears tattered pale robes that flap in the breeze, almost yellow with age and dirt. Its face is covered by a featureless bone-white mask, ovoid and smooth. I try to lift the Beretta but it's so heavy and my hands are trembling. I just want to go to sleep.

***

After I've done my work I wipe the blood from my lips and take one of the last two cards from my pocket: the King of Spades.

But death is not the end, rejoice!
The Pallid One has made His choice.

I place the card in the detective's mouth. The Pallid One stands beside me and whispers His approval. I want to ask Him how He knew the detective would be here, how He knew he'd be alone, how He knew I would succeed—but to ask such questions would only annoy Him, I'm sure. He says He will unmask for me now, if I'll just follow his last instructions. Of course I will. He tells me to take off my clothes. I do. He tells me to take the last card, the King of Diamonds. This one has nothing typed on it. He tells me to put it in my mouth. I do as He tells me and stand facing Him, staring up into that shining oval. My tears are no longer sad. I regret nothing. I am not afraid. I have earned my reward.

He lifts a pair of slender, ashen hands and—carefully, tenderly—removes His mask.

the duelists

HALF A LIFETIME ago, I fought my last and only real duel.

Back then, Arkham had one showpiece fencing event, held over two weekends every spring at Miskatonic University. On the second Saturday night, the final eight competitors squared off on the *piste* before an audience of some two hundred people. A daunting occasion, even for a seasoned swordsman.

The event was conducted in elimination format, with the finalists fencing off in pairs to scores of ten. The winning fencer would receive a cash prize and the top four finalists would move on to national competition.

Having fenced since age thirteen, I felt confident, and soon all that stood between me and the championship was my final opponent, Philip Eden.

Philip, the eldest of three brothers, had studied to be a concert pianist but proved unsuited to this due to a slight webbing between his fingers. His father was a self-made businessman from Innsmouth who specialized in wholesaling fashionable and exotic jewelry to the cheaper end of the market. All three sons went to Miskatonic, all three took up both boxing and fencing with a vengeance, and all three lacked the honor such sports call for. Of the three, only Philip fenced with both foil and saber.

With a foil the target is the torso, and one can score only with the sword's point. With a saber the point may be used, but one is also free to slash, and the target is anywhere above the waist. The saber is the more dramatic weapon, more like what one sees in Douglas Fairbanks pictures. And, like Fairbanks, Eden was an exhibitionist. Off the strip he would dress in black, his shirt unbuttoned midway, revealing a pale, hairless chest on which rested a gold pendant and chain. He often sported a gold bracelet and gold rings of similar design, all with a curious marine motif. He was just under six feet tall, with small ears, a narrow head, a wide smile, and large, dark eyes.

He was talented, with a short fuse: I lost to him often, albeit narrowly, and after one disputed decision I watched him hurl his mask the length of the hall. Eden was also superstitious, fascinated by the occult, and spent hours a day in the university library studying its moldy copy of the rare and fabled *Necronomicon*.

A few weeks before the tournament Eden approached me to "come to an arrangement": the fight would be rigged so that he and I would end the tournament in a draw and split the prize money. What did I think? First, I said, I thought I would win; second, I didn't want to be party to such a scheme; third, I liked the risk involved—all or nothing: the deal was not on. In the following days I learned that Eden was determined to teach me a lesson for my refusal. . There was even talk that he'd cursed me, or charmed his saber, or both. I waved off the gossip.

Three times between then and the tournament I dreamed of a marvelous city, golden in the sunset, with walls and arched bridges of veined marble. Silver-basined fountains sprayed in broad squares and perfumed gardens, and wide streets marched between delicate trees and blossom-laden urns. Mystery hung about it as clouds about a fabulous, unvisited mountain, but as I stood breathless and expectant at one of its temples I was awakened by a throbbing pain in the back of my head.

It was maddening, and by Saturday evening it was difficult to concentrate. I arrived at Miskatonic's Howard Hall, a building of faded Victorian grandeur more often used for lectures and conferences, and made my way round the back of the audience to the rooms put aside for the fencers. Empty, save some discarded clothes—I was the last to arrive. I donned my white breeches and socks, special fencing shoes, and canvas jacket. Glove, mask, and saber in hand, I walked from the changing rooms past a long line of spectators, feeling like a gladiator about to enter the arena.

I stepped up onto the *piste* and did battle amid shouts and applause until only Eden and I remained.

For the final fight we had two judges watching us, one on either side of the *piste*, who would move up and down the strip in concert with us, expected to assess every hit. Controlling the fight and posted mid-*piste* was the referee, whose job was to analyze the action and add his vote on hits.

I saluted each in turn, then my opponent.

"Gentlemen, *en garde*," said the referee. "Are you ready?"

We both nodded.

"Then fence."

All at once I watched Eden's mask, the angle of his body, the stance he assumed. His blade as it arced towards me. I was hyperaware, sensing the audience's reactions while focusing on Eden himself. I thought at lightning speed, deciding upon and taking actions in fractions of seconds, my reactions all but instinctive.

When we changed ends at the halfway point, I found I was leading five-to-one. Maybe to play up to the crowd, Eden was taking flamboyant parries, trying to predict where my blade would land, but his guesses were going wrong and each time I got through. The change of sides, however, brought a change in fortune. Now Eden's guesses seemed telepathic, as if he knew exactly where I had chosen to aim. Four times he parried me, his ripostes whipping through, forcing me to shift tactics. But he advanced fast, launching a long attack through my defenses that landed across my chest. The judges' hands shot up: five-to-six.

I tried to attack again, but Eden stretched out his arm at just the right moment and, rushing forward too eagerly, I ran into his point. As soon as the referee told us to fence again, I attacked Eden's head, but he took a fast parry and, with a loud, triumphant cry, riposted to my mask with such force that his blade whipped over the protective mesh and sliced into the back of my head. Blood spattered my jacket. The whole audience gasped.

The score was five-to-eight: I was down by three hits. The hall seemed hot, and when I put my hand to the back of my head my fingers came away red and sticky. The wound hurt much worse than I would have expected— the pain seemed to permeate my entire skull, and there was an almost unbearable sense of pressure, as though something was trying to get out. I glanced at the audience but saw only one of Eden's side judges looking at me with disgust—as if to convey, I thought, that no one who threw away such a commanding lead deserved to win. Then I noticed the other judges shared the expression, as did many members of the audience—and on most of them, there was terror mingled with the disgust.

I chalked it up to concern or shock over my obvious injury, and resolved to continue the bout despite my pain. I took a small step forward and lifted my saber in an offensive posture, but Eden had stepped back. I couldn't make out his eyes, but it was obvious from the way he stood that he was unsure, even afraid himself.

Before I could ask what was wrong, I felt a tug at the back of my head and something long and thin whipped out from somewhere behind me and struck Eden in the head, knocking off his mask. He raised both arms, batting at the thing with both sword and hand as it continued to strike at him like a snake, and at last the tendril retreated. The pain in my head was unbearable. The audience and judges were still staring, but now many of them were screaming. I could barely stand.

I ran, saber and all. I was aware only of the pain in my head and the revulsion and horror my presence suddenly seemed to inspire. *Whatever had struck at Eden had come from my wound.* The realization made me sick to my stomach, but I was too panicked and disoriented to stop and examine the thing.

I fled from the campus, determined to find solitude. In the streets women screamed, men shouted, and a policeman attacked me with his baton. I brought my sword arm sideways to hold him back, and the blade of my saber hit him hard in the face. He fell, but I didn't even glance back. Something had possessed me, was driving me to flee.

I managed to hide in Arkham's dark alleys and later that night I left the city for good, settling in Billington's Wood to the north. Beneath the pain, fear, and worry of the following days, I wondered if Eden would get the prize money by default. *He* did this to me, the treacherous bastard. The rumors of his witchery were true.

He'd somehow caused me to sprout a long, greenish-gray tentacle with purple markings and a red, sucking mouth on the end. Now, thirty years on, I am sitting in what I've come to think of as "My Wood" with a score of them hanging limp about my shoulders like a Gorgon's hair. They only come to life when in the presence of prey; over the years much livestock has been found dead and drained of blood throughout northeast Massachusetts. I hesitate to claim all credit, though I doubt there is another of my kind roaming the countryside. Horse blood is my—*their*—favorite. I no longer eat solid food. For the first year I got unbearable stomach cramps, in addition to my lingering headaches, but both have since subsided.

It's been a long, wearisome life.

In these woods I lurk to descend upon such victims as might pass my way. Tall trees rise all about, their sullen branches shutting out the sunlight. Dim game trails lead in and out among them. At night, through a rift in the forest, I can see the forbidding lights that hint of the city to the south. The forest seems uninhabited now—deer no longer scamper, birds no longer chirp. My accursed presence has made these woods all but inhospitable. When it's warm I swarm with flies, but in the winter I have only myself to whisper to. What few attachments I had before the tournament are forever severed, though I still dream of that wonderful, mysterious city with its fairy gates and marble terraces. Those dreams are my only solace; I know I'm damned.

The tentacles seem to have a mind of their own. They have directed much of my self-preservation. I think a few of them are developing rudimentary eyes.

I still wear my jacket—now stiff and brown where my blood stained it, and somewhat tattered—though the tentacles and my thick beard have made the mask too uncomfortable. It serves no practical purpose here anyway. I still carry the saber though. With the aid of it and the tentacles I fought off dozens of black bears and coyotes, before they abandoned this country. Men have hunted me too. I can't blame them. I've become a savage, hateful thing. I've killed them, when they're alone in My Wood. None who see me can be permitted to live.

What's that? I hear twigs and leaves crushed underfoot. Something— someone—is coming!

I shift my grip on my saber and quicken my step. I glance about and hide behind a great tree, ready to fight or flee. I peer out and see something emerging from the brush.

Is it...? It is—a man! I haven't seen one in almost a decade.

Some six feet in height, strongly though leanly built, coarsely clad in deerskin. But something is wrong. He moves with a strange, shambling gait, and his narrow, sloping head is completely bald. His skin is covered in scabrous flakes, like a snake shedding its scales, and bunches into weird folds at the sides of his neck. I've never seen such a man! Could it be there is another inhuman monster haunting these woods? Though there is something about those black eyes, bulging from his beardless face. Something I recognize.

He is armed with a hunting bow; a long knife hangs from his waist, and next to it—a competition saber! And there, around his neck: a gold pendant.

Philip Eden, it's you! You've come at last! The years have not been kind. Could this be the *Necronomicon*'s price, or are you plagued by some other malady?

I step into the open. He spots me, and I see wary recognition in his face.

We eye each other, our mutual enmity seething behind closed mouths. We glower—fading degenerates, fierce wanderers, exiles of humanity— while wild ghosts of our feud whisper to each of us.

There is no sound; the forest is silent.

A grim smile crosses my lips. The tentacles stir, awakened by primitive blood-lust.

Eden's unblinking eyes flash. He shakes in the grasp of a murderous ferocity, but there is also fear there. He throws down his bow and touches the hilt of his saber. It appears I'll have another duel yet.

I lift my sword and run to him. My confidence flares and, with a swift whirl of steel, we meet.

the vindication of y'ha-nthlei

I DIDN'T LIKE his face, and I told him so.

It was the spring of 1928 and I was sightseeing in New England. Newspapers were crying about a recent fire that wiped out most of the empty houses and buildings in some ancient waterfront town called Innsmouth, and about a simultaneous explosion that destroyed some reef a mile and a half out from shore. Most papers said arson, but nobody seemed to disapprove. In fact, the few folks who cared at all seemed more relieved than upset, talking about an old brick jewelry factory and some Hall of Dagon or something like that, and saying how good it was that they were gone. One or two papers said government raid, that Innsmouth was lousy with bootleggers and stills, and that the reef was torpedoed to keep smugglers from using it as a drop.

Anyway, I was at a shabby speak in Newburyport reading one of these papers when in walked this man, a damned drunken swine with small ears and bulging eyes and a narrow, balding head. He stank like fish. When he saw my paper, he snorted irritably and muttered something to the effect that Innsmouth was nobody's damned business. There was something bizarre about his vocal timbre that made me uncomfortable. I told him I'd never even heard of the place until three days ago, and he cussed at me.

"You'll all get yours," he said. It was then I noticed the scabrous-ness of his skin and the loose wrinkled folds on his neck. I'd heard some locals call that the "Innsmouth Look." So, he'd probably just lost his home, or his business, or both, and had every excuse to be mad—but just then I didn't care.

I'm a reasonable guy, most of the time, with the understanding that we're all God's children regardless of race, language, or appearance. But I'd had a few myself and this guy was funny-looking in a different way. Nobody would ever call him handsome, but more than that, he seemed downright sinister. I could tell most of the people in the bar shared my unease just by looking around. There was an unnatural curve to the corner of his mouth, more pronounced now by the involuntary twitching of his upper lip; a warning that a man is half-seas over and getting to the stage where he'll slop, which is not my business—unless that man decides to slop on me.

"I don't like your face," I said, feeling mean and satisfied to get it off my chest. "In fact, I was going to drive to Rowley tomorrow, but I think I'll go tonight so I won't have to look at you any longer."

The Innsmouth man growled and cursed away to himself.

"Let him be, now," the bartender said. "His temper will work itself off."

"Miserable sluggard," I said.

"He's as the Lord created him," the bartender said. "But why He did it, I don't know. Those damned Innsmouth fellers got it in their heads to spread all over New England now, except now they don't have that jewelry people were so mad to spend their money for. People will sure be keeping their eyes open for that stuff, now the factory's gone."

Here the Innsmouth man waved his hand and mumbled something indignant. The bartender went on: "I hear some Innsmouth folk are finding work on fishing boats, diving for pearl-oysters. Say what you want about their looks, they can dive more than fifty fathoms deep. Not entirely hopeless, if they don't mind a little adventure. I hear they're as comfortable in water as out, even the women."

The Innsmouth man blew into a sky-blue handkerchief and went on cursing to himself.

Suddenly he moved closer to me.

"You don't like my face, eh?" His pale-blue eyes stared, unblinking. The rough skin on his forehead contracted and formed little ridges all the way up to the wispy blackness of his receding hairline. The quivering lips turned into a sneer. There was something unnatural about that leering, threatening face. The stink of fish and booze was overwhelming.

I leaned back against the bar.

"Why don't you just crawl back into the water?" I said.

It occurred to me then that he might be carrying a gun. I can draw a little quicker than most men. Course, being quick on the draw's not much when your revolver's in the car outside.

I moved down the bar, pretending I didn't see him follow me; also ignoring the bartender's pantomime, which was to indicate to me that I was holding a Roman candle in my hand, with the wrong end up. Which was sound advice—but I didn't fancy the bartender butting into my affairs.

"You're a smart guy, ain't ya?" The Innsmouth man's elbow crooked on the bar and his uneven cheek went into his own coarse palm. "Private investigator? A dirty dick? And you don't like my face. Well—a lot of people don't like to see it. They've got cause to fear it." He paused a moment, licked at his lips, sort of smiled unpleasantly to himself—then his unblinking eyes glared at me like an animal, his lips slipping back.

"Well—it's ugly enough," I told him. "Why don't you take it downtown and use it to frighten policemen?"

"Yeah—yeah?" He didn't seem the sort of guy who went in for light banter. "Yeah?" he said again, and then, "You read the papers. Wonder what they really found in Old Man Marsh's factory? And below Devil's Reef? Wasn't just sharks, by Hydra. Best be careful with us Innsmouth folk—you could die."

He'd been half-mumbling so far, but his voice was loud now, and others were listening. His hand shot up and fastened on the lapels of my coat. He jerked me straight—he was surprisingly strong. He kept talking, and his voice took on a slopping quality that gave me the shivers. "Your kind will pay for sticking their noses where they don't belong."

"If you don't want that face of yours even more mussed up, why, take your dirty hands off'a me!" People were gathering now. There was a chance for him to pull back, but he didn't take it.

"Face mussed up!" he repeated. He must've liked his twisted map. I tried to jerk free, but he held on tight—he was so strong—and threw open his coat with his free hand, let me see the gun beneath his armpit. "You'd like to think you have the guts to cross me?" A slight pause as he shoved his face closer, making me gag with his fish-and-booze reek. "Well—"

I pasted him. Maybe I lost my head. Maybe I didn't. Certainly, though, there was nothing definite in my mind when I let him have it. I had nothing in my mind but his glaring eyes and protruding chin and quivering lips. If I had any desire at all, it was to shut his foul mouth—and perhaps that's even stretching the truth a little. The desire, after all, was just to sock him.

He let go and stumbled back a step. He wasn't hurt—just surprised and drunk. I landed another punch right on his nose and he hit the floor.

I jumped over him and left before he could reach for his gun. "I'll kill you! I'll kill you," he shrieked after me, in a dazed sort of way. But I was already at my car.

I decided to cut my sightseeing short.

***

Three years later I was on a honeymoon cruise with my new wife, Anne, whom I'd met in Chicago after my return from Newburyport. She was something of an heiress—her father owned a paper company—and had been largely insulated from the Great Crash, but that's not why I married her; I'm no four-flusher, never have been. Mostly, it was love. Real love, the kind you don't expect to see outside storybooks or Janet Gaynor pictures. We'd fallen hard for each other, and even her bluenose parents couldn't deny the truth of it.

It was eleven at night, and we were some thirty miles west of Cornwall aboard the ship *Guinevere*. The cruise had taken us on a tour of the Celtic Sea to Ireland, Wales, Devon, and Cornwall, and was now on its way back home to America. We were leaning on the rail, taking a breather. From the saloon came the sound of the dance continuing, and the crooner asking, "What is this thing called love?" The sea stretched in front of us like a silken plain in the moonlight. The ship sailed as smoothly as if she were on a river. We gazed out silently at the infinity of sea and sky. Behind us the crooner went on baying.

"I'm so glad I don't feel like him; it must be devastating," Anne said. "Why, do you suppose, do people keep on singing these dreary songs?"

I had no answer ready for that one, but I was saved the trouble of trying to find one when her attention was suddenly caught elsewhere.

"What's that?" she said.

I looked where she pointed at a small spot among the still, moonlit waters, and with some surprise. Something was sticking its head out above the surface to look at us.

"A fish?" I said.

We regarded the creature for some moments.

"It seems to be coming closer," Anne said.

We went on staring, and it came quite close. "There's another one," Anne said.

Sure enough, there was: another head, a little smaller, a few yards to the right of the first. "And *another*," she said. "To the left. See?"

She was right about that too, and by this time the first one was keeping pace with the ship in our slow wake.

"They might be some kind of dolphin," I said, and shrugged my shoulders as casually as possible, though I didn't believe it myself. I could see the thing's ugly mug now. It was a pale, grayish green and completely bald, with a narrow head that shined wetly in the bright moonlight and a wide, froglike mouth. But worst of all were its eyes—bulging, dark orbs that never seemed to blink.

I'd overheard some talk among the ship's crew about increased sightings of "sea devils" in recent years, but those half-remembered snippets were only secondary in my mind to a strange familiarity that both fascinated and repulsed me. These scaly monsters looked almost human, in their way.

We watched all three of them slowly getting closer, leaving little wakes of their own in the water as they approached ours.

"Five now," said Anne. "What are they?"

Others were leaning over the rail, and they appeared to have seen the creatures too. Now there were eight of the things, nine, a dozen...

I shivered with sudden terror. The closest of the creatures had reached the edge of the ship, and now out of the water stretched an *arm*. Not a fin or a tentacle, but an all-too-human arm, ending with a long, webbed hand. With this it pawed at the side of the ship as though it intended to *crawl up*.

The rest of the things continued their approach. There was time for people to go back into the saloon and fetch their friends out to see, so that presently a line of us leaned all along the rail, looking at them and guessing:

"Did you ever see anything like that before?"

"Devils from the sea!"

"There aren't any devils. Those things must be some kind of fish or something."

"A fish hasn't got any hands, sir. I went to school..."

"Didn't Beebe see something like that in his bathysphere?"

"Three fishing ships lost in the Pacific last year, two more off the coast of Iceland..."

They looked about man-sized, as far as we could judge. All we could be sure of was that they were crossing our wake and descending on the ship in a long, crooked line.

My wife looked from me to the creatures. It wasn't a memory that would linger pleasantly in her mind. I wondered if I should get my gun from our cabin.

Now the first creature pulled itself out of the water, anchoring itself to the side of the ship with claws or suckers or whatever was on those big hands. Then, swiftly, its companions spread out along the ship's sides and followed suit. They were indeed of the approximate size and shape of a man, with two arms and two legs and a total height or length of about two meters.

Then they spoke.

They were beginning to climb up when the croaking sound of their voices reached us. It was an articulate speech, but one I'd never heard the like of, full of frothy hisses and barks. They kept repeating something that sounded like someone half-belching the syllables *ee-ha-nith-lay*.

I decided we were in immediate danger. The crowd sort of fell back, and I took the opportunity to retrieve my gun. It was just a .22, and I had no idea if it'd prove deadly against these giant fish-frogs, but having it made me feel bigger, more in control, and it took the edge off my fear.

By the time I got back, the passengers were scrambling all over the deck with desperate haste, and the first fish-beast was already clambering over the rail.

"Clear the way!" I yelled, and shot it in the face. It jerked back with a hiss like steam, but those huge, webbed hands clung tight to their perch. Another shot sent it tumbling back into the sea. The second of them came up, in just the same way, in almost the same spot. Five of them climbed up in total, one after another, only for me to send them back to the water with great whooshes. Then I was out of bullets.

And they were still coming, fast.

Bells clanged, the beat of the engines changed, and we started to change course. The crew turned out what few weapons there were to be had—fewer than a dozen firearms between them and the passengers, myself included, and not even a full spare load for each. Some men carried wrenches and other tools as makeshift clubs; one passenger even had a bayonet.

There wasn't time to organize all the able men. The monsters were boarding from all sides, and they didn't wait. Soon it was an all-out brawl. Some of them carried long knives that looked like whalebone.

One of them, clutching such a knife between its teeth like a pirate, stood out a bit from the rest. It was naked and bald, like the rest of them, but stood a bit more erect, with skin that was less scaly in patches. There was something familiar in its hard, cruel face, with its fishy lips and bulging eyes a little smaller than those of its brethren.

The Innsmouth Look.

The memory hit me like a brick.

The man from the speak!

I think he saw me, but I can't be sure. At least, he never looked straight at me. I stood back in the shadows while he went by to gut some poor sap, slicing the guy open like a calf in a slaughterhouse. I wanted to vomit.

Fingers fell upon my arm. I whirled, my pistol raised like a club.

It was Anne.

"Come on," she said. Her voice was soft, but her face betrayed her terror. "We have to hide!"

I nodded. She could see as well as I that it was useless to get mixed up here. The boys were fighting bravely, but the devils were still boarding, and as soon as the bullets ran out the tide would turn fast. I followed Anne back through the narrow halls to our cabin. I don't think anyone saw us, but being inconspicuous wasn't our highest priority just then.

We've been here all night. The fighting ended long ago, but we can still hear those croaking voices and the shuffling of webbed feet. I wonder if they intend to scuttle the ship. We can't be the only ones left. Someone else must've lasted this long, must've hid like we have. There were hundreds of people aboard. I only saw a few dozen of *them*—but who knows how many more crawled up since we abandoned the massacre?

Now I stand with my back against the cabin wall, Anne in my arms, and through our small porthole the sea looks placid and empty in the fuzzy morning daylight—but I know now what flounders beneath that unperturbed surface. If the captain radioed for help, it hasn't arrived. Perhaps our would-be rescuers met a similar fate.

Are we witnessing the beginning of humanity's end? I'd rather not think so. I'd rather wake up from this nightmare, finish my honeymoon, and eventually tell a kid with Anne's freckled looks and my unusual last name about the time Dad had a bad dream full of sea monsters.

It does no good to cry over what we never had, but I do anyway.

I hear a noise at the door, as of many slippery bodies lumbering against it.

"God," Anne screams. "The door! *The door!*"

It buckles, and creatures tumble in with a reek of fish and a chorus of gurgles, the Innsmouth man among them. Anne cries in my shirt and I hold her tight, unable to look away from my boogeyman. He looks straight at me this time, and I see recognition in his face as he raises his bloody whalebone knife and closes the gap between us.

"*Get yours,*" he croaks.

in their reeking talons

THERE ARE PEOPLE who collect stamps, and others books. For many years Mr. George Howard Karel, despite collecting both, had found no real meaning in his life. For a long time, he hesitated between an interest in prehistoric burial places, a passion for foreign politics, and a familial obligation toward the study of zoology—particularly waterfowl. The evening of the Nantucket Horror, however, it dawned upon him suddenly what had been lacking in his life to make it full and complete. Great things are usually unexpected.

Even though he, like most of the world, was unaware of it until that day in 1936, the invasion had begun long before. Actually, as had become more and more apparent to Mr. G. H. Karel in the fourteen years following Nantucket, it was more *reclamation* than invasion. Not the imposition of a *new* order so much as a revival of the very, very old. *They* were here first, after all.

Instead of stamps or books, Karel now collected newspaper clippings about the Deep Ones. His zeal as a collector preserved much material which otherwise would have passed into oblivion. He cut out and put away anything in print about the Deep Ones that he came across. In the first year after Nantucket, before coffee became a rare and expensive import, Karel learned in his favorite St. Louis coffeehouse to ransack the papers whenever the Deep Ones were mentioned. He became skilled in unobtrusively tearing out the page and whisking it into his pocket under the waiter's nose. Like most collectors, he was prepared to steal if it meant adding to his collection. Also like most collectors, he did not believe this lowered his moral character in the least.

Now Karel—wearing a stiff, broad-brimmed hat over his wispy hair; a cheap blue suit over his wiry frame—sat at a forward angle on the green plush train seat, looking one minute at the window as if he might want to jump out of it, and the next down at the handful of clippings arranged in his lap. The train raced through treetops that fell away at intervals and showed the sun standing, red, on the wooded horizon.

"I think the early evening like this is the prettiest time of day," the woman facing Karel in the section said. She had a faint Mid-Atlantic accent, and Karel wondered briefly if she was a stranded Briton. "Don't you think so too?" She was a pink, pear-shaped woman, with legs that didn't quite reach the floor. She'd been reading a worn-out copy of *Show Boat*, but now the open book rested face-down in her lap.

She pushed her glasses down and looked over them at him, noticed the clippings in his lap. "Oh, dear…" She leaned back in her chair.

He looked at her a second, leaned forward with a shrug, and stared down at the clippings again, wide-eyed.

He imagined he must by now have an encyclopedic knowledge of the Deep Ones. His collection filled two large shoeboxes in his bag, leaving only a little room for the empty gun and his other personal effects. He even had a few documents in other languages—Cyrillic, Greek, Hebrew, Arabic.

He poured over the handful in his lap with pious reverence, murmuring the headlines to himself.

ARMY LOSING GROUND DAY BY DAY

ROOSEVELT BARRICADES COASTAL STATES

JAPAN AND U.K. AMONG ISLAND NATION CASUALTIES

BORDER WALLS PROVE INEFFECTIVE

GARNER ASSUMES PRESIDENCY

U.S. CAPITAL TO MOVE INLAND

EX-SIGNALMAN DRAMATIZES NANTUCKET BATTLE IN NEW FILM

SHOGGOTHS SPOTTED IN OHIO

"I—I guess you're going home," the woman said, turning back to him again.

"No earthly good, talking to me," he said without moving his eyes from the clippings. "There isn't a sane person that'd touch me with a forty-foot pole, except to do me harm."

Karel did not include in his clippings either the name of the source or the appropriate date, so in most cases he didn't remember when and where this or that statement was printed. Furthermore, with the overwhelming supply of material available, he chiefly preserved long articles which he considered to be the most important, while brief notes he simply threw away after reading. When his boxes became critically full, he silently and surreptitiously pulled out some of the clippings and burned them, a procedure that took place several times a year. He only spared those which were uniquely rare, like the ones printed in foreign languages; these remained preserved almost in their entirety. The material he had at hand concerning the history of mankind's interaction with the Deep Ones was, in consequence, quite fragmentary.

He looked up and found her squinting at him, red-faced.

He turned toward the window and then almost as quickly turned back again to the clippings.

"You'll probably be contaminated if you associate with me," he said coolly. "In most countries I'd be under arrest by now."

"Terribly disappointing for you," the woman said in mock pity. "This has always been discouraging territory for ambitious martyrs. But you do try, don't you?" She looked at the clippings in his lap again.

Karel caught her look. "I'm a collector," he said.

"I see."

He gave her a glance and saw the flat of her face, still reddish under a cap of fox-colored hair. She'd got on two stops back.

She couldn't leave it alone. "Those horrible monsters have ruined the world."

"If not them, then probably someone else would," he said. He bent a thoughtful, disapproving look on her.

She looked away half-sulkily, not answering him.

He lit a cigarette and looked at her for a moment, then shook his head. He folded into a slouched position and settled one foot on a pipe that ran under the window.

He looked at the clippings sourly and gripped his hat by the brim.

"What I want to know—" the woman began.

"Going to Chicago," he cut her off and ground himself into the seat and looked at the window. "Don't know anybody there, but that's where I'm going."

The woman said she knew a man who lived in Chi...

He wasn't listening to her anymore. Out the window he saw a vast, dark sphere rolling over the landscape, faintly glowing in the diminishing sunlight with greenish pustules that winked on and off.

A 'goth! Karel had never seen one so close. This one was larger than the train car—and it was bearing down on them. Fast.

The woman saw it too and fell silent. She snatched at her collar, the red leaving her face.

The car was full and other people were seeing it too, pointing and screaming. Karel and the woman were the first to stand up, but they were immediately knocked flat as the train rocked with a sudden impact. The clippings fluttered like startled gray butterflies. Karel looked at the window and saw only a mass of glistening green eyes against utter blackness. The woman was unconscious. He almost got up before another tremor felled him.

***

When Karel came to, the sun had gone down and someone was dragging him uphill along a gentle grass slope. He looked up and saw a black-haired man, straining in the pale moonlight, gripping him by the wrists.

"What...?" Karel said.

Noticing that he was awake, the man dropped Karel's arms at once and ran past him, back down the hill. Karel followed him with his eyes to the train below. Eight of the eleven cars were derailed, and people were littered along the side of the track in loose heaps. Karel couldn't tell how many were dead. The man who'd rescued him was darting among the bodies like a carrion bird, looking for the jerk of a hand, the twitch of an ankle, any movement that might indicate a salvageable person. Karel lay on his back for a few minutes and didn't move. There was something spongy in his throat with an eggy, acid taste. When he finally choked it back down and looked around him he saw three youngish women: the black-haired man's previous charges, he figured. Two were unconscious, the third was sitting up and looking at the wreck, glum and intense. She looked at him with small eyes, saying nothing. He lurched to his feet and put a hand to his head to quell his immediate dizziness. His hat was gone and his hair was matted, and his fingers came away dark and sticky. There wasn't much pain.

"Jesus save us," the small-eyed woman said. She turned back to the wreck.

"Do you think I believe in Jesus?" Karel said, leaning toward her and speaking breathlessly. "He wasn't on that train. He wasn't who spared us."

He drew back, followed her gaze.

The black-haired man was trying to help someone stand, a teenage boy. From between two of the derailed train cars stretched a limb of iridescent black slime, thirty feet long and thick as a tree trunk, with myriads of glowing green eyes rising and sinking on its surface. It swept man and boy off their feet, crushing and absorbing them before withdrawing back between the two cars.

Karel sat down hard on the grass. It was still here. Of course! Now that he really looked, he could see the faint green glow of its eyes rising above the train cars and passing through the windows. It had flattened itself out on the other side, probably feeding; around one corner another heavy, dark limb curled, quivering idly over prone bodies, eyes pulsing. A brisk

Midwestern wind brought up a stealthy purring noise, like the sound of shoaling undertow.

He thought about the clippings. His record of the Great Reclamation's progress.

All gone now.

For an instant he imagined lurching down the hill, recovering what he could. Perhaps the 'goth would recognize him as a servant of the Order. Perhaps it would spare him...

No. It was utterly indifferent to his efforts, to his dedication. To his existence at all. He saw that now. It had attacked the train, after all. His own survival was pure chance.

There was no protection against these terrible, shapeless monsters. The Deep Ones held no leashes after all, or else they didn't care to use them to protect their human followers.

He realized at once that the only difference between the Order and the rest of ignorant, desperate humanity was that its members had recognized their impotence early. If they couldn't beat the Deep Ones, they'd survive by joining them—except the amphibious things had little use left for allies or servants.

It would devour me like any other.

He laughed a little at the realization, not knowing why. His arms shook with a nameless black mirth. His hands continued shaking long after the laughter subsided.

The small-eyed woman's mouth jerked down as she watched him, but she said nothing.

He lay back down in the grass and watched with her, noticed the 'goth's amorphous limbs curving around to the near side of the wreck. It looked as if it might come this way soon. He lay there for a while, not moving. In the distance beyond, further down the railroad track, he could just make out the lights of Chicago. He thought of his preacher grandfather; his wealthy alcoholic father, the professor; his two younger brothers. All dead or estranged long before Nantucket fell. After a while he was almost asleep, with the small-eyed woman still sitting up next to him.

she said she was a magic mama

ALDERMAN TONY MASON walked up and down his living room on dark, windy, gentrified East Street. Mason was a fat man, with dark eyes and two chins. The fingers of his right hand splayed around a glass of Chianti, from which he gulped at frequent intervals. His left hand hid in the pocket of his tobacco-brown pants. An expression of worry wore his face like a suit.

The winter night wind keened in the street outside and shook the windows. Mason stopped short in his pacing as his five-year-old daughter bowled into the room wearing pajamas emblazoned with teddy bears.

"Night, Poppa."

Mason put down the Chianti, but he did not pick up the child and bounce her up and down, as he usually did. His left hand remained in his pocket.

"Goodnight, Angel," he said.

His wife came in, smiled, and picked up the girl.

"I'll take her," she said.

"Yes, Mama," Mason said. "Put her to bed and then close that door. Captain MacDonald will be here any minute."

"You want to be alone, don't you?"

"Yes, Mama."

She looked at his left arm, at his pocket. "It's about…"

"Yes, Mama. Please take Angel to bed and then you, too, leave me alone."

"All right, Tony." She looked a little sad.

He laughed, and his ragtag mustache fanned over his mouth. With his right hand he pinched his daughter's cheeks, then his wife's, then marched with her to the inner door. They went out, and he closed the door and sighed.

He went over to the table, picked up the glass of Chianti, and marched up and down the room. His broad, heavy shoes thumped on the carpet. The floor creaked.

When the bell rang, he fairly leaped into the hallway. He snapped back the lock and opened the door.

"Ah, Cap! Good you've come!"

MacDonald strolled in wearing a neat gray overcoat. His hands were in his pockets and he smoked a cigar.

"Slow at Headquarters, so I thought I'd come down."

"Yes—yes—yes."

Mason closed the hall door, snapping the lock. He bustled into the living room, eyed an old recliner, then took a couple of pillows from the couch, placed them in the recliner, and patted hollows into them. He did this all with his right hand, and then spread said hand towards the chair.

"Have a seat, Cap."

"Thanks."

"Give me your coat."

"That's all right, Tony."

MacDonald merely unbuttoned his coat and sat down. He was freshly shaven and combed, and his long face had the hard, ruddy glint of one that knows the weather. He leaned back, crossing one finely creased leg over the other.

"Chianti, Cap?"

"A shot of scotch'd go better."

"Yes—yes—yes!"

Mason brought a bottle from the sideboard, followed by a bottle of Canada Dry.

"Straight," MacDonald said.

Mason took one with him, taking forever to bring the first to MacDonald before going back for his own.

"Here's how," he said, and they drank.

MacDonald looked at the end of his cigar.

"Well, Tony, what's the trouble?"

The wind clutched at the windows. Mason went over and tightened a latch. Then he pulled up a rocker to face MacDonald, sat down on the edge of it. He stared vacantly at MacDonald's polished shoe.

"About my—curse," he said, finally.

"Hm."

"Look, Cap, I'm a good guy. I'm a good man. I got a wife and a kid and a chemical waste business and I been elected alderman and—well, I'm a pretty good guy. I don't want to be on no racket, and I don't want any kind of help from any rough guys in the neighborhood. I got a wife and a kid and a good reputation and I want to keep the slate what you call pretty damn clean. Cap, I ask you to come along here tonight after I been thinking a lotta things over in my head. I need help, Cap. What's a man gonna do when he needs help? I dunno. But I know you do things for the aldermen sometimes. So I ask you, and maybe you be my friend."

"Sure," MacDonald said. "Get it off your chest."

"This woman—uh—Cave, Samantha Cave."

"Uh-huh. What about her?"

Mason took a long breath. It was coming hard, and he wiped his face with his right hand. He cleared his throat, took a drink, cleared his throat again.

"Her. It's about her. Her and my—uh—curse. You know she's only twenty-one. And—and—"

"Going around with Cave, were you?"

"Yes—yes," Mason's voice was a harsh whisper as he shot a worried glance over his shoulder. "Look. This is it, and Holy Mother, if Dominique knows—" He exhaled a vast breath and shook his head. "Look. I have lotsa needs, Cap, being what I am, a complicated man. I have lotsa needs, some big, some not that big. Sammy—uh—Cave, she met my needs a few times, as recently as last night."

MacDonald uncrossed his legs and put both heels on the floor. He leaned forward, resting an elbow on one knee. His windy blue eyes stared point-blank at Mason.

"And?"

"Well—" Mason sat back, eyes wide, and spread his right hand palm-up. "She cursed me, I say!"

"How long has this been going on?"

"Maybe a month."

"And this curse?"

Mason fell back in his chair like a deflated balloon. "That's what you call it, Cap. We were very good friends. I thought Sammy was a great girl. She must think I'm an old fool."

MacDonald looked at the floor, and his eyelids came down thoughtfully; the ghost of a sardonic curl came to his wide mouth.

Mason hurried on: "Look, Cap. My Dominique is a good wife, but if she finds out I slept with that—that *whore*—it's gonna be no good. I can't stand for it, Cap. And what can I do with Sammy? She's laughing at me, the greasy witch, with those dreadlocks and tattoos and the metal through her nose and those little tits of hers. Dominique has done nothing bad, but Sammy—"

"Where does the curse come in?" MacDonald asked.

Mason looked at the ceiling reluctantly, and withdrew his left hand from its hiding place with a sudden jerk.

But it wasn't a hand. Protruding from Tony Mason's left sleeve was a muscular, mucous-covered tentacle. Gray-green and shiny, it seemed to flex and move almost automatically, and was covered with what looked like rudimentary suction disks on one side. MacDonald stared at it for a long time in perfect silence, his cigar hanging limply from his mouth.

"Every night I went out with Sammy, she ain't got the money, so I pay all the bills. And where do we go? Ah—the Club Nowlan, and places like that, and that woman—Holy Mother, it ain't good, Cap! Last night we were at the Nowlan and she gave me something."

"Gave you something? Like scabies?"

"Little square of white paper, less than half the size of a postage stamp. No taste. Said it was acid, but it didn't do anything. Should've known it was a trick when she didn't charge me for it. Anyway, when I woke up…"

He held the tentacle forward. It probed the air as if sensing for something. As if it had a will of its own.

"Jesus," MacDonald said. "Have you spoken to a doctor?"

"No," Mason said. "I haven't been out of the house all day. And what could a doctor do, anyway? Besides, I've got my reputation to think of." He paused, and when he spoke again he was on the verge of tears. "Look, Cap. Whatcha think I'm gonna do?"

MacDonald's gaze had not left the tentacle since Mason had revealed it. Now he looked the fat man in the eye.

"I think you're going to have me kill this woman."

Mason made a nervous, uncomfortable face.

"No, no," he said. "I need her to fix this. I need you to find her and make her fix this."

"What if she can't?"

Mason grimaced again. "Then…you know."

"Know what? You need to be clear."

The fat man was sweating. "Do what you thought I was gonna have you do."

MacDonald nodded slowly and sat back. He was silent for a long time, staring at the tentacle.

"Hell, Tony," he said at last. "I've had a lot of tough jobs in my day, but you hand me … I mean you've got my sympathy, and that's no bullshit. I'll get started tonight. I'll do the best I can."

"Please, Cap, please. My wife and my baby—I ask you, Cap, for my sake."

"Sure, Tony."

MacDonald stood up.

Mason stood up, his breath whistling in his throat. "But if Dominique finds out—"

"She won't," MacDonald said. "Not from my end."

He buttoned his coat and shoved his hands into his pockets. "I'll be going."

"Have another drink."

"Thanks—no."

Mason let him out into the street and hung in the doorway.

"Night, Cap."

"Night, Tony."

MacDonald was already swinging away, his cigar a red eye in the wind.

***

From behind the bedroom door, Dominique Mason heard the front door close and the lock snap, heard her husband's creaky footsteps, heard the soft *whump* of his bulk settling on the couch.

Things were turning out even better than she'd hoped. Now not only did she know the identity of her husband's mistress, but Sammy Cave was going to be punished as well—and this time Dominique wouldn't even have to collect hair clippings from the trash, or light that stinky incense in the attic, or chant any more of those awful things from that horrible black book she'd ordered.

As for Tony, that lying monster—his transformation had only begun.

***

The sound of her husband's screams woke Dominique up with a start. He had fallen asleep on the couch and never come up to bed, which was just fine as far as she was concerned; she'd been dreaming about a candlelit dinner date with Jeff Goldblum. But now the dream was over, and her husband was awake.

Tony was standing in the living room, shirt and tie discarded on the floor, clutching with his right hand at his left shoulder, which was now the base of a very long, very muscular gray-green appendage that hung down past his knee. The tentacle writhed gently on its own, its suction disks now fully formed, strings of mucous connecting it to Tony's pants and naked torso where it made contact.

He was still screaming.

"*Tony!*" Dominique said. She wanted to tell him to shut up, tell him it wasn't even 4 a.m., the sun hadn't even begun to rise, that he'd wake the baby. But then she remembered the role she was playing, and forced a sob. "Oh, it's terrible!"

He hardly seemed aware of her presence. *Typical.*

She ran to him, careful not to get too close—not to get within reach of *it*—and sank down crying. It wasn't all an act—she *was* upset, but *at* Tony, not *for* him. But this was getting a little more drastic than even she'd expected; she'd thought the transformation would stop just after his elbow—sort of a blasphemous take on that "if thy hand offend thee" verse from the book she *hadn't* had to order. Just what Tony deserved.

But the tentacle was already quite a bit longer than his whole arm had ever been, and she saw the folds of skin around the base of his neck had already taken on that shiny gray-green color. His screams had subsided, but his hair and moustache were moist with sweat, and his rapid breathing had taken on a strange sucking quality. He remained standing in place, still clutching at his shoulder, the tentacle still twisting slowly and constantly against him, but his eyes looked vacant, and his legs trembled.

This was too much.

Dominique waited a little while, looking at her husband, watching him with mounting unease, and finally ran back upstairs to the bedroom telephone.

It rang only once before someone picked up.

"Thanks for calling MU Press's twenty-four-hour customer service line," a young woman's voice answered. "This is Sammy, how can I help you?"

"Yes, hello," Dominique said. "I ordered a book from there not long ago. *Necron*-something by, uh…oh, I don't know, some Arab name, I think. It's a black textbook."

"Yes, ma'am, I know what book you mean." The young woman was professionally polite, though her tone was now a bit more clipped. "We get a lot of calls about that one. It's actually why we had to extend our business hours."

Tony's sucking breaths grew louder below. Still holding the receiver, Dominique went over and closed the bedroom door as softly as possible.

"I used it to…um…cast a spell," she said, almost whispering. "On my…husband."

"Yes, ma'am?" The young woman let a hint of bored incredulity slip into her pro-friendly voice.

"Well, I tore up the page when I was done, just in case he found the book—but now I think I want to undo the spell."

"Counter spells, where applicable, are located on the opposite side of each page for easy access—"

"I just told you, I tore the page up!"

"Yes, ma'am." A slightly annoyed edge this time. The silence that followed seemed to say, *What do you want me to do about it?*

"Well, is there something else I can do? Some other way to reverse it?"

"One moment, ma'am." Not even hiding the contempt this time.

Little bitch.

She heard movement outside. A gentle knock on the door.

"Mommy?"

Angelica.

"Go back to bed, baby," Dominique said. "Go back to bed right now, please."

"Okay, Mommy."

Tiny footsteps receding. It occurred to Dominique to lock her in her room, but just then the young woman's voice came back.

"Ma'am?"

"Yes, I'm still here."

"I happen to have another copy of the book here in the office with me. Can you tell me which spell you used?"

Dominique thought about it. Once the spell had been cast, she'd tried to put the weird syllables as far out of her mind as possible. They'd made her feel unclean.

Downstairs she heard movement; the creak of Tony's weight mounting the stairs.

"Ma'am?"

"Um…not the exact name, no."

"How about the page number?"

"I can find that—" Dominique began, then swore under her breath. She'd hidden the book in the attic with the intent of burning it after Tony learned his lesson. He was nearing the top of the stairs. "Uh, can you hang on just a moment?"

"Of course, ma—" the young woman was interrupted by a voice from her end of the line.

"Sammy?" it said. "You have a visitor."

Dominique stifled a gasp. The woman's name hadn't registered with her before, but now—

She heard Tony's footsteps stop just outside the bedroom door, his rhythmic, sucking breath louder than ever. Then he moved on.

Where is he going?

"I'm with a customer," Sammy said, not bothering to mute or muffle the phone.

"I think he's a cop," the other voice said. "Says it's urgent."

That was the last Dominique heard.

Angelica was screaming down the hall.

Dominique jumped and ran into the hall, dropping the phone. Spots of mucous on the left side of the carpet and wall left a trail to the little girl's bedroom, where the door stood open into darkness. The child's cries had already given way to a horrible gurgling noise.

She approached the room more slowly than she'd intended. *Just go*, she thought. *Your daughter's in there!* But the sickening noises gave her pause; try as she might, she couldn't force her feet to move any faster.

Reaching the threshold at last, she could just make out the shape of her husband's bulk—no, not her husband's, not anymore—standing over Angelica's bed, his back to the door. Was *he* making those awful sounds?

With a trembling hand, she turned on the light.

And took her turn to scream.

the worst

ROBERT BELKNAP, WHO at twenty-three had sold a whopping four short stories in five years, never expected to find any further degree of fame until he entered middle age.

But that was before he received an email from a man at the *Providence Periodical*.

He was a finalist in the newspaper's international Lovecraft contest, and as such was being invited to read his work at an event celebrating Lovecraft's birthday. His girlfriend agreed to make Providence the sight of their one-year-anniversary vacation and, on a hot day in August, they made the sixteen-hour drive in Sharon's car. They could only afford to make it a four-day weekend, and he wanted to get there early.

He'd spent hours practicing his reading—the story was quite short, not even two thousand words, but he wanted to make sure he paced it just right: the mounting dread as the little boy found an ancient grimoire in his grandfather's library, the dawning terror as he accidentally summoned a brooding, bloated monster…

"What's the worst thing you've ever done?" Sharon asked from behind the wheel.

They'd crossed into Connecticut almost an hour ago, after the boring stretch through Pennsylvania and the brief horror of New York City. They'd exhausted most avenues of casual conversation and all agreed-upon listening options: NPR, some mutually acceptable CDs—The Beatles, Chicago, Elton John, Hall & Oates—and the entirety of *The Hitchhiker's Guide to the Galaxy*. They were saving *Life of Pi* for the return trip.

"Probably cheating on my ex," Robert said.

"No, that's not it," Sharon said. "Tell me for real."

"Not bad enough?"

"Not to you," Sharon said. "Or you wouldn't have told me on our third date."

"Fair," Robert said.

"So, what's the worst thing?"

"Okay. Remember when I told you about the time I ran away from home?"

Sharon nodded. "You were thirteen, your parents were getting divorced, your mom found you walking along the road that day."

"Right," Robert said. "We were out in the country."

"So?" Sharon said. "You were just a kid."

"Before Mom found me," Robert said, "I went under this bridge about a mile from our house. Sis and I used to go there sometimes to watch the minnows. I'd brought my backpack with—"

"A sleeve of saltines, the *Official Boy Scout Handbook*, ninth edition, and *Taggerung*."

"There was another book!" Robert said, losing patience. "Just forget it."

"No, tell me," Sharon said. "I'll be quiet. Please?"

Robert sighed. "This book was one I'd taken from my grandpa's house up in Wisconsin that summer. It was small, like a diary, and bound in alligator skin, but it must've been really old because the pages were yellow and stiff and the spine was reinforced with duct tape. There was no title—"

"Come *on*," Sharon said. "You've been practicing all week. It's getting dark and we're five states from home. I'll make you drive through New York on the way back."

"It's true!" Robert said. "Where'd you think I got the idea?"

She frowned at him a moment, then conceded with an almost inaudible "okay" as she looked back toward the road.

"I had this book," Robert went on, "and it was all hand-written in another language—I have no idea what. There were little strips of paper pasted onto some of the pages with words typed in English. Rhyming couplets, but not like Shakespeare or anything. These didn't make *any* sense. I guess they were translations."

He paused, looked at Sharon. She was focused on the road, but glanced back at him when he stopped talking. "Some of the strips were typed phonetically," he went on. "Like pronunciation guides. I tried a few of them out, but the sounds felt...I don't know...*wrong* coming from my mouth. And that's—" He paused again, steeling himself for the revelations to come.

"That's what?" she asked, concern in her voice. Was she starting to believe him?

"That's when something moved in the water. I was sitting on these rocks right on the creek bank. I was barefoot, dipping my toes, when I saw a splash. Too big for a minnow. I thought it might be a frog or a turtle, but then…I…" He reached out and took a gulp from the soda he'd bought at the last gas stop. "I realized it was nothing."

"Nothing?" Sharon sounded almost relieved, almost disappointed.

"*Nothing*," Robert said. "A sort of *void* in the water, like something invisible standing on the creek bed. And then it *moved*, and…oh, God…"

"What?" Sharon asked. "What did it do?"

"I saw these little five-toed footprints press into the mud, one after the other. There were only two…they were almost like *hands*. And there was a groove between them, like maybe a tail or…*something*."

"What happened?"

"I ran." Robert gulped more soda. "Left the books, crackers, even my shoes and socks. Mom found me walking barefoot about an hour later. Guess I'd calmed down some, 'cause I didn't tell her much. Just that I'd left my shoes by the bridge. Guess I was ashamed."

"Ashamed of what?"

Robert looked at her. "I *summoned* something that day, with that book, just like the kid in my story. When Mom took me back to get my stuff, the book was gone. And then the accident…"

"So?" Sharon said, incredulous again. "What's that got to do with it?"

"I was so mad at her when I was under that bridge," Robert said. "Her and Dad both. I just remember *hating* them when I was reading that book, almost *wishing* something bad would happen. And then it did, and Mom had no idea what she hit, but it snapped her front axle in half and left some sort of weird slime all over the grille. Thank God we weren't hurt, but I just remember thinking it went *after* us."

Sharon spoke with the tone of one trying to calm a mental patient. "But if she hit it, that means it's dead, right?"

"I thought so," Robert said. "But then those animals wound up in our yard…rabbits and squirrels, torn to pieces, just like in my story—"

"Sure it wasn't a wild dog?"

"The last one was a deer's head—just the head—with the eyes and tongue missing." Robert shuddered in his seat. "Dad thought it was some sick teenagers, but the security camera he installed only ever caught raccoons. Anyway…" He looked at Sharon. "Bringing that *thing* into the world is the worst thing I've ever done. It's kept me up more nights than anything, and I regret it so much that I've never talked about it with anyone before. The End."

They were both silent for a long time.

"What about your grandpa?" Sharon asked at last. "In the story the monster kills the little boy's grandpa."

Robert shrugged. "He never missed the book and I never had the nerve to bring it up. Now he's been dead almost six years, and unless you consider a stroke a monster…" He trailed off, let out a long, satisfied sigh. "Guess it was time to talk about it. Maybe that's why I wrote it down this year." He smiled at her. "Thanks, I guess, for asking."

"You're welcome?"

"I mean it. Good to get it off my chest."

He touched her knee. She smiled back at him.

A few minutes later they passed the sign they'd been waiting for:

WELOME TO RHODE ISLAND
THE OCEAN STATE

In the strengthening dark, neither of them saw the grass part on the side of the road ahead. Or the muddy, five-toed footprints that stamped across the pavement—one-two, one-two—before stopping in the middle of the lane.

hairworm

IN THE DUSTY, black hours of the town, the drifter walked in the lees of walls, in alleys, in abandoned lots like a lean, feral cat. No other soul stirred in the grim brick perimeters.

It was cold. The drifter slapped his numbed hands together, then stopped for fear of drawing attention. His heart thudded his unrest, not accounted for by the chill night air or the long, fatiguing walk from the farm. He'd eluded his pursuers, but the sharp *clip-clop* of iron-shod hooves still echoed in his ears.

He moved through an old cemetery surrounded by thin trees, a small metropolis of curious stones where names and crosses dimmed with time. He felt the damp earth through the leaky soles of his shoes. He continued down little sandy streets where neglected cars sulked, crossed the clay-banked railroad where weeds sprouted between the ties. A solitary engine coughed like a lion in the distance as he crept between broken streetlights, past chain link fences, down ruined sidewalks, under wires that bellied pole to pole across the constellations. As the sky lightened with the coming sunrise he prowled into a dirty public restroom. He washed his face and mouth in the sink and, with water still dripping from beard and fingers, sat down at last on the floor of the farthest shit-smelling stall.

Within his skull drifted a nameless certainty of his own permanent solitude. No one would ever believe what he'd seen at the silo.

***

Tom's door opened almost before Barry's knock, and there he was standing in the dark with a small parcel wrapped in brown paper under his arm.

He smiled and said, "Come in, Bare, and take off your coat."

Barry went in, and Tom locked the door behind him.

Tom was Barry's college roommate who'd dropped out to join the army. He'd been discharged for forging a paycheck and was now back in town and working at a local radio station in order to, as he'd put it on the phone, "cultivate a smooth, affable manner." Affability, however, did not come natural to him. Barry recalled that, in repose, his expression had always been sullen and mean. He still had that mean expression, but it was softer now.

"Well," Tom said, seizing Barry in a tight half-hug. "It's good to see you. What's it been, three years?"

"Thereabout. I'm glad you called."

"Yeah, so I gathered. You been crying, man?"

Barry winced, bracing himself for the inevitable teasing. He had been crying when Tom called. Sitting and crying in the cineplex parking lot.

Tom held up a hand. "It's okay. No judgment."

Barry looked at him.

"Yeah?"

The movie, a coming-of-age dramedy about a teen girl's turbulent relationship with her mother, was a critical darling for its realistic depiction of parent-child conflict and love.

But Barry wept from envy. Envy of the easy closeness the main character shared—and was able to display—with her female best friend. Their genuine platonic intimacy at school, at the friend's home, at prom…it was all so unfair. Barry couldn't remember experiencing such unabashed closeness with a male friend since the earliest years of grade school. Sometime before junior high it had all dissolved amid shouts of *no homo* and a constant need to reaffirm masculinity. By high school's end they'd all been so afraid to touch each other—unless it was a playful arm-punch or back-slap, something aggressive enough to avoid looking too sensitive—or talk about anything other than girls' bodies or the latest action movies and video games, that the old closeness was all but forgotten.

It all came pouring out of him then. The starved longing, the sense of invisible isolation—of being utterly alone even among friends, each man an island in a scattered archipelago.

And Tom listened like a true friend, asking questions without interrupting or dismissing. Occasionally he broke in with vague exclamations of solidarity, punctuated by wild gesticulation. He seemed to have adopted some strange new points of view, but would not elucidate on any of them. Perhaps they'd always been there, had only sharpened in his time overseas. Whatever he was thinking, he seemed energized. Empowered. Like he'd found religion or something. It was during this long conversation, sometime after Tom had invited him to stay the night, that

Barry realized just how long he'd been stewing in his own rudderless dissatisfaction. And how much he'd missed having Tom in his life.

"Here's what you need," Tom said at last, and opened the brown paper parcel. Inside was a small clear-plastic bottle, the size and shape of a miniature liquor bottle, but without any label. It was filled with a colorless liquid that might've been water or alcohol, and at the bottom, coiled in a loose knot, was a small yellowish worm no thicker than a piece of thread.

"What is this?"

"You hear of mezcal worms? Like that, but more exceptional. You swallow it whole, and it dissolves in your entrails. Makes you feel good, down in your bones. Makes you feel like a man."

"Where'd you find it?"

"Russian pal gave me one in Europe. I was going to sell this one, but I think you could use it."

Barry took the bottle, opened it, smelled its contents. He detected a faint fragrance of licorice, but that was all. No alcohol smell.

"I don't know…"

"Remember when we dropped acid sophomore year?" Tom asked, almost talking to himself.

"Yeah. Nothing happened and we never got our money back."

"You only need to do this once."

"You have, then?"

He nodded. "I don't even smoke pot anymore."

"You mean it's *permanent?*"

"Not in a bad way," Tom said, raising his hands in a placating gesture. "It's a subtle improvement."

Barry gently swirled the bottle's contents, hesitated. He *had* missed this—hanging with Tom, living through his reckless eyes, if only briefly. Tom had always had a way of talking him out of his comfort zone.

"I don't know…"

"*Trust* me, Barry."

It *did* feel good, being persuaded into something new and illicit.

Barry shifted his legs under the kitchen table and stared at the worm. It had a vaguely phallic head and might've been two inches long when not coiled up. It didn't move.

When *was* the last time he'd done *anything* illicit? Hell, anything *new?*

He sipped at the bottle; the liquid had a mild, spicy flavor, but was otherwise indistinguishable from water. Then he tipped it back and swallowed it all in a few gulps. He didn't feel the worm slide over his tongue or down his throat, but when he sat forward again and looked, the bottle was empty.

Tom stood, smiling. The dark of his shadow slipped over the table.

Barry felt nothing. Then he felt cool, like a nice breeze had just hit him. Then he felt sick. He ran to the bathroom.

"*No!*" Tom followed, shouting. "*Don't vomit!*"

He seized Barry's shoulders in an iron grip and wrenched him away from the toilet bowl, throwing him against the near wall with surprising force.

"What the f—"

"Keep it down," Tom said. "It'll get better in a minute."

Barry sat against the bathroom wall, his back aching where it'd hit the edge of the doorframe. Already he could feel the nausea subsiding.

Tom extended a hand, calm now. "Sorry," he said, pulling Barry to his feet. "Just—these things are expensive."

"Sure," Barry said.

"You okay?"

"Yeah, fine. Am I supposed to see something holy yet? I don't see anything."

"No hallucinations, just feeling. Sit and relax a minute."

"Okay."

Tom watched Barry resume his seat at the kitchen table, as if afraid he might rush back to the toilet, and then left his sight. After a moment, Barry heard the melancholic sounds of The Sisters of Mercy pulsating from the other room—an old mutual favorite—and resigned himself to await the transcendent ecstasy Tom had promised.

Instead, in the following hours he felt only solitude—but an enjoyable, almost spiritual solitude. No sensations or feelings at all other than that of being an island universe unto himself, and without the crushing loneliness that had always accompanied such for the past two years.

***

Waking up on Tom's couch, Barry felt magnificent. Redeemed, like Lazarus emerging from the tomb. Over a breakfast of eggs and tea he felt tethered to Tom as by a fine, invisible thread. Tom formed the sole exception to his solitude, allowed only because he shared it.

It was how it'd felt in college, amplified tenfold.

A hazy restlessness filled his mind. While Tom sat motionless, watching him silently from across the table, Barry sipped his tea, looking toward the window. It was a dark day, overcast. The sort of weather that always sharpened his loneliness and left him mired in depression.

Or, rather, always *had*.

He shook his head and stared down at his crusted shoes, caked with the debris of life. The stuff of the cosmos, he reflected: matter; yet somehow spirit. A stuff more fundamental, more primal, that he was only beginning to understand.

"How do you feel?" Tom asked, observing him closely. His voice was almost a whisper, as if he were afraid of disturbing some delicate balance.

"Like you said," Barry said, still staring at his shoes. "More or less."

"New man?"

Barry shrugged, nodded.

"That mean I can trust you?"

"Yeah, of course."

"Good. Let's take a little drive."

"A drive?"

"Yeah," Tom said, moving to the door. "A few of us have started gathering every week at this homemade observatory a few miles out of town. Converted grain silo, pretty cool stuff."

"Us?"

"Yeah, some friends. We look at the stars, pet the horses. We're trying to bring more guys in."

"Into what?"

"Just *in*. You'll get it. Come on."

***

They stopped at a neglected 24-hour gas station on the way, with only two pumps and an inattentive, white-haired woman behind the register. "I've got to use the toilet a minute," Tom said, as Barry browsed the snacks. He'd almost decided between sweet and salty when he heard a loud commotion from the restroom. The elderly cashier didn't react at all, engrossed in an issue of *Ellery Queen*.

Barry went in.

Just outside the farthest stall, a bearded, jowl-faced man in a squashed hat stood over Tom, a bloody length of pipe clutched in both hands.

Tom was belly-down on the floor, his skull crushed, his limbs twitching as the blood pooled around him.

No, not just his limbs, his whole body below the shoulders. And not just twitching...

The hips arched and sagged, Tom's corpse miming a grotesque copulation with the floor. The entire torso tensed, then slumped, and Barry saw something long and thick snaking its way down one leg of Tom's jeans.

The old man, Tom's murderer, watched with Barry, the pipe all but forgotten in his grip.

The thing extended the length of Tom's leg, emerging from the denim over the heel of his shoe. It was dark and yellowish, and thicker than the fat end of a pool cue. Its head was vaguely phallic.

It slithered out onto the floor and wound its way blindly between the old bum's legs. The vagrant just stared with wide, rheumy eyes, as though witnessing his own most ludicrous and terrifying tin-foil-hat conspiracy theory vindicated before him. Tom's torso deflated, an emptying husk, as the worm continued to emerge. It was eight or nine feet now, still coming out of him, smearing in his blood as it writhed free.

Barry ran outside, into the parking lot, and vomited. The cashier didn't look up from her magazine.

When the heaves subsided, he studied the puddle of half-digested eggs and tea. Nothing moved in it. He ran his fingers through the warm puddle, hoping to sift out something solid, something about two inches long and narrow as a piece of string.

It's got to be here. It can't still be inside me.

But Barry knew it was even before he withdrew his fingers from the mess on the pavement. He shuddered, tried to vomit again, but nothing else would come.

Too late.

A peculiar placidity rose up and settled over him almost at once, so abrupt and overpowering that he hardly noticed its strangeness.

It was okay.

He was okay.

Untethered from Tom, the rudderless isolation remained at bay. The invisible thread remained intact, pulling in a new direction. He still belonged *somewhere*.

Barry stood, got into his car, and started driving.

He didn't have Tom to guide him to the observatory, but he no longer needed Tom. Deep down, Barry already knew the way.

Something in his gut told him.

a gator we should turn to be

WAS IT ONLY today the Witch turned up in Jacksonville to weave a net she thought could hold us? Late that morning—this morning?—we took Elaine—the name she gave—on the boat through the calm, green waters of the Atlantic and hunted south along the coast for a sandy beach where we could rest and swim and drink Coke.

She was a tall girl with long legs and a slight limp. She wore a blue bathing suit, cut high at the firm thighs, snug over the slender curve of waist and small breasts. We knew she wasn't a tourist. It wasn't just her limp, or the recent scar on her right shoulder; it was a bad feeling from deep down in our socks, almost a stink in our nostrils as she handed us the wrinkled ten-dollar bill from her sunflower purse for the boat ride. We added a few bucks to the usual price, hoping she might leave us alone, but she would've paid twenty or more before letting us go. We took the money and let her aboard. Gotta be crazy to do otherwise on such a hot, dead morning, right? That's how it'd look.

Marvin Gaye started singing on the transistor radio we kept in the boat: "Stubborn Kind of Fellow." Elaine was telling us about a concert she saw two weeks before in Miami.

"Elvis and John Lennon have nothing on Jim," she said. Faint Midwest accent—Wisconsin, maybe? Hard to tell if you've never been north of Georgia. "I mean, he was stumbling around the stage, guzzling beer, squinting at the audience. But he looked so tough with that devilish beard and dark shirt, those black leather pants…"

She noticed our copy of *Tales of Gooseflesh and Laughter* where it sat next to the radio, with its weird rocket-ship structures on the cover, and asked if we'd seen the Apollo launch. We hadn't.

"Author just died," we said. "Wanted to catch up."

She pulled a hardback out of her purse to show us what she was reading: Raymond Chandler, *Killer in the Rain*. Blue jacket, with a knife like ours next to the title. It reminded us of the young boys on the train tracks, their flesh roasting over our fire, steaming in the light December drizzle. Mr. LoScalzo hadn't hired us for that one; that one had been just for *us*.

We chose a curved, narrow piece of island three or four hundred yards from the shoreline, edged the boat into the beach. Elaine slipped over the side into shallow water to guide the keel against the white sand. She did this without asking or being asked, like she'd done it before.

We'd decided not to kill her, though we wondered if she had a death wish. We yawned, though we weren't tired. It never hurts to throw them off, even if you don't throw them overboard. *The Feeling* can come upon one at any time.

"You want me here, don't you?" Elaine asked suddenly, her thick, dark hair hitting her shoulders. Her eyes were wide open as if she were seeing us for the first time. She was staring at us; we had her complete attention now. "I mean, I paid for the ride, so I might as well hang, right? Anyway, I could use some company."

Testing us. She had to be in her early or maybe mid-twenties. The kind of young woman to drive us crazy on curious days, especially when The Feeling comes with its mild shakes and its strange, familiar sounds.

The radio played Donovan's "Season of the Witch."

She smiled, but not in her eyes. The muscles in her long legs tensed; the left was scarred below the hip. We wondered how her bones might look.

"Your name's not Elaine," we said.

"Names change," she said, after a moment's hesitation. She reached into her purse, for the weapon we knew she'd hidden there; a switchblade, a can of Mace, perhaps even a small pistol. "Your name isn't Roger."

"Names *are* interchangeable," we said, chuckling in spite of ourselves and fingering the knife in our pocket. We'd almost forgotten which name we'd given her.

"Where is Phil Carmody?" she asked.

This name was familiar. One of the ones Mr. LoScalzo gave us. Months ago, even before the boys.

"Who sent you?" we asked the Witch.

"Someone who knew Carmody," she said. "Someone who doesn't like your associates in Tampa reaching this far north."

We'd have to kill the Witch after all. She was a wild young woman, probably a drug addict or an alcoholic, not dim but not as bright as *us*, almost certainly a sociopath. Someone had hired her to "straighten us out," as Mr. LoScalzo might say. How much were we worth? $20,000? $50,000? Anything less would be insulting.

We would cut the nose off her face, strip the flesh from her long legs.

We would eat her, like the boys.

She was already taking something out of her purse, but we were bigger, probably faster…

We rushed her like a reptile, swung out with the knife.

She ducked and brought the gun up: a small black pistol.

***

We wake on the beach at night, feeling like a shaken Coke bottle.

We are alone. The boat is gone, and with it the Witch, the radio, the knife… The air is warm and damp. Our skin itches from the sand. Our head hurts.

We push the heel of our hand against our head, brush loose a few grains of sand, and feel a familiar stickiness. The Witch's bullet grazed our skull just above and behind our eyebrow, but didn't penetrate. The skin there is ragged and torn. We've lost a lot of blood.

We look out to where boats sail in the dark, lights reflecting on the still water. A gull calls from somewhere.

We sit up, hands shaking. We are alone. Our heart hammers. Our eyes sting. Behind them, burnt there, we still see the flash from the Witch's gun.

We must try now. We can make it.

We can hold our breath a long time.

The water of the Atlantic stretches out before us, gleaming with the million lights of the city in the distance. The voice of the deep is seductive, constant, inviting us to wander in a black abyss of solitude.

We leave our clothes on the sand and stand naked in the open air, at the mercy of the gibbous moon and the beating breeze like a newborn thing.

The gentle wavelets curl up to our feet, coil like tentacles about our ankles. We walk out. The water is cold and deep, but we walk on, lift our bleeding body and reach out with a long, sweeping stroke. The sea's touch is sensuous, enfolding us in its soft, close embrace.

We go on and on. Don't look back. Just go on and on and on. One of the boat lights is brighter than the rest.

Our limbs tire. Our head stings and aches.

We think of the Witch, the boys, Mr. LoScalzo, but only for a moment. They are no longer objects of concern.

Exhaustion presses us to stop. The shore is lost in the light, the boat (*is it a boat?*) so close now.

We can hold our breath a long, long time.

We look into the light. Terror flames up for an instant, then sinks again. We hear our ancestors' voices. We hear their dead, croaking language.

We can hear Atlantis, full of cheer...

like nothing you've ever seen before: toeing the depths of izzy reeves

AN AMPHIBIOUS MONSTER bites off the top two-thirds of a man's head.

And that's just for starters.

It rips out his spinal cord too. It makes crunchy, slurping sounds as it eats him. Its slow, thumping crawl belies the sudden speed with which it leaps onto its prey. The young couple watches the old man die with looks of insane horror on their faces, the final realization dawning that they have found themselves transported into a kind of hell. And you, the viewer, begin to realize it with them. The creature's long, muscular tail may not have a barb at the end, but its spiny caudal fin, gorgon-like external gills, and tough, onyx-black skin are demonic enough. Not to mention those neck-ripping teeth and glittering, deep-set eyes. It is terrifying to imagine, horrifying to behold.

Isadore Anglemyer Reeves was suffering one the unhappiest spells of his short life when he began writing *Children of Ceto* in 1961. On a personal level, he was still recovering from a failed marriage, of only eight weeks, to his high school sweetheart. And professionally, he was distraught from having been harshly rejected by his favorite director, Eugène Lourié, after attempting to become the French monster maestro's assistant cameraman a year earlier. One can only imagine how differently things might've turned out.

It's no mistake to call Reeves a prodigy. Devoted, obsessive, and single-mindedly ambitious, the Brooklyn-born filmmaker wrote and directed brilliantly effective feats of horrific imagination as early as age thirteen. The short films made during his teenage years—now considered lost—were said to be works of such visionary extremity, they had the power to raise (or raze) one's consciousness like a tab of acid. No one else has ever possessed Reeves' warp of mind, and nowhere is that clearer than in this vision of prehistoric sea-gods made flesh.

By the time its monster has been revealed and explained, *Children of Ceto* has not exhausted its material but instead gotten a second wind. With effective camerawork and revolting special effects, it sets the stage for what must be the goriest, grossest, and bleakest climax of the 1960s: an outrageous caveman-style battle against not one but two of the ferocious beasts—dubbed "Sthenosaurs" by the film's Dr. Gordon, after the eldest sister of Medusa. When one is successfully stabbed, it makes an evil hissing sound as it bleeds that is downright stomach-turning.

Make no mistake; this isn't a Lourié-style science fiction film, though some of the classic Hollywood monster trappings are there if you can spot them: the old loner scientist/entrepreneur who discovers an unknown or thought-to-be-extinct creature on an uncharted island and seeks to study/exploit it for his own uses, only to find he's underestimated the danger involved. He goes too far, and he suffers for it. Reeves' screenplay doesn't shy away from the influence of Merian C. Cooper and Jack Arnold.

But where *Children of Ceto* defies expectations is in what happens to the rest of the people involved. In a more conventional film, the remaining characters would cooperate, confront the danger, kill or at least evade the monsters, and go on in their own restored world. In love, most likely.

Not here. Here, the survivors descend into madness, rape, and murder before the ruthless final scene. It is bizarre pulp horror executed with a stark realism that makes it all the more suspenseful and frightening. The small cast is made up of complete unknowns who have never appeared in anything since, removing even the small comfort of a familiar face or voice.

Also removing, perhaps, the certainty that this is just a movie.

The film was shot on an island in the North Atlantic, though Reeves never disclosed the exact location. The special effects are phenomenal to this day. Where other monster films of the decade would utilize stop-motion animation, or men in rubber suits, Reeves' methods for bringing his Sthenosaurs to life remain a tantalizing mystery, much like David Lynch's deformed child from the decade following. One might be forgiven for first assuming they are optically enlarged lizards made up with gills and fins, *a la* the earlier adventure films of Henry Levin or Irwin Allen. However, by Dr. Gordon's death scene this assumption becomes impossible to maintain. One common speculation is that Reeves obtained a pair of adult Komodo dragons, painted them black, and glued on the additional extremities. However they were done, the creature effects—as well as the intensely believable gore—rank among the best of any period.

Reeves never publicly acknowledged *Children of Ceto* as a major achievement, and it rates barely a mention in his surviving journals. Yet at the original film's first and only public screening, in April 1966, he was by all accounts beaming proudly during his introductory remarks. And despite the film's violently negative initial reception and the director's apparent reticence, several decades later the sheer raw purity of the film, and its powerful narrative thrust, confirm *Children of Ceto* as one of the highest peaks in surreal exploitation horror.

Even if some of the dialogue is corny and the characters are formulaic (one available man, one available woman, one driven scientist…), the script as a whole is functional and tight, all the while pervaded by an oppressive sense of doom. Under Reeves' fine direction, the actors make us care about the characters. They become interesting, even compelling. The blend of horror and documentary realism becomes seamless in the latter half, when the movie goes beyond formula to a gravely determined and inventive stance of its own. *Children of Ceto* has the courage of its monster, a monster it knows is worth putting front and center. It also has the courage of its ideas and simple premise, which is just realistic enough to keep the film from ranging into the preposterous. The film intrigues and frightens because its urgent tone and inevitable escalation are so firmly grounded in this dangerous, twisted world that it refuses to become dated.

The collision between mankind and nature revealing the savagery of both runs as a leitmotif throughout. Mankind's wanton and reckless treatment of the natural world is symbolized by the sinister, almost expressionistic way Dr. Gordon is shot in his early scenes, and by Kate's furious trampling on the gleaming white bones of a dead Sthenosaur later in the film. The opening shots of the trio's boat alighting at the island are framed—both by the cinematography and the score—as a hostile invasion. The close-ups of the island's sparse trees and trickling stream, backed by ominous music, suggest that the humans are interlopers here. Unwelcome, and soon to be dealt with.

This is one of only two feature films that Reeves directed. The second, *Artois*, an epic historical drama set during the final years of the Seventh Crusade, was plagued by a troubled production. Though principal photography was completed in 1970, the film remained unfinished at the time of Reeves' mysterious death in January 1971, mere days before his twenty-ninth birthday. What footage survives reveals considerable inner tension—alongside moral and psychological ambiguity—in what is ostensibly a straightforward thirteenth-century adventure. It is difficult to imagine how different the cinema landscape of the 1970s and '80s might have been had Reeves lived to realize his full potential.

Following the disastrous spring premiere, a censored 73-minute version of *Children of Ceto* opened in select theaters in June 1966. (This Blu-ray edition includes both the censored version and the complete 76-minute original.) Audiences were still repulsed, and after its brief limited release, the picture closed for good, becoming only a memory in the minds of the few who saw it. A nightmarish figment.

Until now.

anatomy of a broiler oven

OCTOBER 29, 2:59 A.M.

The rain had stopped. Brent and Brian sat on the porch, looking out over the street to the park beyond. The smoke from Brent's cigarette drifted into the cool, dark sky. It made Brian cough.

"It's Darren, sis," Brent repeated into his cell. "I'm not sure—I'm not dreaming it. *I* haven't been drinking, I said it looks like *he* might've been."

Brian sighed. A long, high, shuddering sound.

"His hands," he whispered. "His *eyes*."

"Yes," Brent said into the phone, puffing on his cigarette. "No. No, I haven't called a doctor. I don't know what a doctor would do…"

***

October 28, 11:12 P.M.

Electric stoves—or "broiler ovens," as he'd called them for years, thanks to Mom—had always made Darren uneasy. He disliked the way the broiler element was planted at the top of the oven, just out of sight. It was a downright hazard.

Darren's mother had a gas stove in her house—formerly his house too, before he'd moved into the small apartment below his uncle's. During the move she told Darren how lucky he was to not have to worry about deadly leaks. He conceded that she had a fair point, but in two years he'd still only used the oven a handful of times. Usually at Hannah's insistence.

He'd get no more insistence from her though. Sooner or later the question comes up in every relationship: How often does the status quo need to shift in order to prevent stagnation? Different lovers answer the question in different ways, but in Hannah's case the ideal time for a shift had already come and gone. His reluctance to move out of his little apartment annoyed her. He'd still been living back with Mom when they'd started dating, just after college, and Hannah—having already been on her own four years before that—had been eager to move in together after year one.

No matter what Darren did, in spite of his sweetness, in spite of his sincerity, Hannah would not be satisfied living alone in the same apartment she'd had for some six years now; the same apartment that wouldn't allow pets and had walls so thin you could hear every squeak of the neighbor's bed. She was ready to start making a home with someone, while Darren still felt he'd only just left his mother's.

"I'm done waiting for you," she'd said at last, when it was lease time and he'd suggested she give him just one more year. "If all you care about is having your little bachelor pad, you're welcome to it."

This had merely been an effort to make Darren see how serious she was, but the suggestion of an ultimatum had so enraged him in the moment that he'd told her to get out.

She had. And hadn't come back.

Two months had passed, and Darren felt washed up. He paced the apartment, his own little island, from end to end.

He wanted something to eat. Wanted pizza.

He'd subsisted entirely on takeout since Hannah had left. There was no shortage of restaurants in town that delivered: Chinese, Korean, Vietnamese; sushi, noodles, deli sandwiches, hamburgers… But Darren's favorites were the pizza joints: Slice, Rafters, Manolo's, Jet's, Rosati's, the list went on and on. There were more of them than all the others combined. One, Vito's, was right across the street from his building. He always ordered delivery though, never pickup. Hannah would've freaked at his laziness, his wastefulness, but he didn't care. That's why he did it, in fact, now that she was gone. He even ordered every pizza with black olives—not a topping he particularly liked, but one that Hannah had always *hated*. He'd eaten more pizza in the past two months than he had in the preceding two years, putting on almost twenty pounds and patronizing every pizzeria in town—even the inferior corporate chains—at least once.

None of them, however, delivered after 11 p.m.

Darren took a long sip from his tall vodka tonic—his third and strongest of the night—and put it down hard on the coffee table. Some of the drink slopped up and over the side, running down to form a liquid ring around the base of the plastic Medieval Times cup. Darren watched it, the light from the TV mirrored in the clear little puddle. If he looked hard, he could imagine a tiny, distorted Raymond Burr there. A homunculus twin of the version on the screen.

It was the screen's fault that he'd waited this long to eat. In the first week post-Hannah, Darren had engaged in some frivolous retail therapy with the complete DVD box set of *Perry Mason*, an old favorite of Mom's and one of which they'd often watched reruns in his childhood. The set had cost over a hundred dollars, and he'd been binging episodes nightly for over a month now, along with a couple of beers. Tonight he'd gotten particularly invested in the marathon, and upgrading to vodka—a response to finding one of Hannah's old hair-ties in his car that afternoon—had only dulled his internal clock. Now he was ravenous and left entirely to his own devices.

He stomped into the kitchen. The freezer held a trio of flat pies wrapped in cardboard and plastic: one pepperoni, one four-meat, and one thin-crust basil pesto that Hannah had wanted to try. The four-meat was the oldest, a Tombstone from the previous Halloween, with a vaguely Italian-looking Frankenstein's monster gumming a slice on the package.

Darren chose the four-meat and closed the freezer door.

In college, his roommate, Seth, had introduced him to an unfussy eatery called Joe's, down in Olney. "The best pizza south of Chicago," Seth said, and he was right. Huge, deep dish, with a sauce so sweet and a crust so perfect there was no need for appetizers, sides, or dessert.

A thin, frozen Tombstone wasn't Joe's, but then nothing in Champaign County was Joe's. Darren made a mental note to visit Seth again soon. They could live it up like they used to, now that Darren was single again.

He set the oven to 400 degrees Fahrenheit and went back to the living room while it warmed up. He downed the rest of his drink, shuddering at the final gulp, and watched the ending of "The Case of the Velvet Claws" before returning to the kitchen and unwrapping the pizza.

"Place directly on center oven rack," Darren read aloud from the back label. He opened the oven, wincing at the blast of hot air in his face, and took the naked pizza gingerly by the crust. It was very cold, and he could sense its extreme fragility.

The oven gaped before him like a mechanized hellmouth, the air inside shimmering like a desert mirage. He bent at the waist, leaning over the lowered door, and extended the pizza carefully into the stifling maw.

It was too hot. Darren felt a twinge of panic and let the pizza go an inch above the oven rack. His hands shot up as it landed—

—and collided with the red-hot broiler element.

"FUCK!" It was more animal cry than word.

Darren pulled his arms close, hands splayed over one another as though he meant to cast some spell. The contact had lasted less than a second, but the pain was unbearable.

An angry, red wound glared up at him from the back of each hand, like a pair of sightless eye sockets. Or stigmata. It certainly *felt* like nails in his flesh.

The pain had seized him like a hand on the collar, jerking him partway out of the vodka haze. Almost immediately, he began to sink slowly back. The pain was still there, only obscured, but already bearable enough that Darren could think of other things. Like what to do about his hands.

Clean. Cover.

He ran to the bathroom, turned on the cold water with trembling fingers, and let it trickle gently over his wounds. The pain surged back up for an instant, but the coolness felt good. After a moment Darren withdrew and hunted under the sink for disinfectant and bandages.

There was only a brown bottle of hydrogen peroxide and a box of narrow Band-Aids too small to cover anything larger than a paper cut. Darren grabbed the peroxide, unscrewing the top and remembering how his father had liberally drizzled it over scrapes in his childhood, often causing more pain than the initial injury but assuring a crying Darren that it was for the best. He remembered somebody—maybe Hannah—telling him how it actually wasn't a good idea to use hydrogen peroxide on open wounds, but he couldn't remember why and anyway screw anything Hannah might've said, this was all he *had*.

He poured carefully to cover each burn, grimacing at the new stinging flares of pain and the way his flesh seemed to bubble. But when it was over, the pain receded back behind the tolerable fog, and Darren felt he'd done right.

But he still needed bandages. And ointment.

There was a Walgreens just down the street, a five-minute walk. Not a 24-hour store on this side of town, but open late. Midnight. Darren darted back to the kitchen, checked the microwave clock: 11:34.

Plenty of time.

It was chilly outside, but no way was Darren going to try putting on a jacket. He grabbed his keys and his wallet, slipped on his worn-out sneakers, and locked the door behind him.

As he started down the sidewalk in the dark, it began to rain. Sprinkle, really. Darren ignored it. By the time he got to the Walgreens, his hair was slightly matted and he could smell what he realized was his own BO, undiminished by the water. It was a strong smell. A greasy, garlicy smell.

He walked straight to the first-aid section without acknowledging the cashier, grabbed tubes of Neosporin and aloe vera cream, a box of large waterproof Band-Aids, and a roll of medical tape. The cashier frowned at him but said nothing other than the standard "This all for you?" and "Have a good night."

It was raining harder on the way back, the grease-garlic smell sharper than ever. The walk felt longer this time. Darren wobbled on his feet, stumbled more than once with his plastic Walgreens bag dangling from one loose fist. Each time he caught himself before he fell, and each time he wondered why he felt so weak, so *soggy*. It wasn't raining *that* hard.

I'm not that *drunk.*

Back in the apartment, Darren went to the bathroom and dumped the bag's contents into the bowl of the sink. He looked at his hands. The wounds still throbbed with every heartbeat, but the pain wasn't so terrible anymore. The skin surrounding each burn looked pale and almost melted. The burns themselves were a meaty, glistening red. They gave off an odor, distinct from the strange BO but somehow complimentary to it. Even, somehow, *familiar*. Darren held his hands close to his nose and sniffed.

Yes, the new smell was unmistakable.

Pepperoni.

Darren shook his head in disbelief, looked in the mirror to make sure he wasn't going crazy.

And almost recoiled in shock.

His face was greasier than ever, with colorless new pimples rising from his forehead and cheeks like little goose eggs. He leaned closer to the mirror, put his fingers to one, and squeezed. A whitish-yellow substance oozed out like toothpaste. Wiping it away, he held his fingers to his nose and sniffed again.

Mozzarella.

"What the fuck?" he said aloud.

Am I going crazy?

His stomach rumbled, as if in response. He realized he still hadn't eaten.

He thought of the pizzas in his freezer, the dozens of delivery pizzas he'd consumed in recent weeks.

"You are what you eat," he murmured, and suppressed a laugh. If he laughed he'd lose his mind for good.

Darren was abruptly aware of how alone he was. How helpless he felt. He needed to talk to somebody. Somebody he knew, somebody who knew *him*, who could tell him he was sane, tell him he'd be okay…

He had to call Hannah.

He fished his phone out of his pocket with two fingers, careful not to brush the back of his hand. Her number was still listed in his contacts, as were most of his exes. Even the ones from high school.

The phone rang.

His stomach rumbled again.

"Darren?" She sounded groggy. "What do you want?"

Hearing her voice again quickened his pulse, dried his throat.

I miss you.

His whole body felt hot, like the oven. He wondered if he had a fever.

"H-Hannah," he said, unable to speak above a whisper. "I—something's happening to me."

"What?"

"I…" Darren began, glancing back to the mirror. More weird pimples seemed to bubble up before his eyes, weeping clear-yellow grease and forming cheesy whiteheads. He could feel them forming on his shoulders now too, under his shirt.

How could he even begin to explain? "Um…I don't know, uh…"

"I can't hear you," she said, her voice edged with an exasperation Darren recognized. "Listen, don't call me in the middle of the night like this."

She hung up.

Darren slipped the phone back into his pocket, stared at his hands. She wouldn't have believed him. He wasn't sure he believed it himself. He was just drunk. Drunk and hungry, and maybe a little delirious from the pain and shock of the burns.

Shouldn't have called her.

That was it. Not crazy, not sick, not—

(Changing.)

Just drunk, delirious. Hungry.

Lonely.

His vision blurred. Tears pushed tracks through the grease, slaloming around the pimples.

His stomach rumbled.

When he bit into his knuckles, the skin gave under his teeth with the consistency of fresh-baked dough.

***

October 29, 3:14 A.M.

Margot's Toyota pulled up, headlights blazing, and was barely in park before she jumped out and slammed the door.

"Where is he? What happened? Where the hell *is* he?" She was already in tears.

"Inside, sis," Brent said, standing and stomping out his cigarette. "The key, Brian?"

Brian handed Brent his master key. He didn't get up, didn't turn his head. Just stared at the grass and sighed again.

Brent led Margot inside to Apartment 1, repeating the story as he unlocked the door. His hands trembled. "I smelled burning pizza and tried calling his cell, but he didn't answer. I came down and knocked, no response, so I woke up Brian..."

Margot pushed past him inside as he opened the door. The living room light was on, as was the TV, frozen on a *Perry Mason* DVD menu.

"There was a pizza in the oven, and it was open," Brent continued. "I shut it off, but the pizza's still in there. That's when I found him..."

Darren was on the bathroom floor, propped up against the open door. The floor was covered with a bright red substance that Margot knew had to be blood.

But it's so thick, she thought. Too thick. It formed a wide puddle around Darren's still form, was smeared on the door and on his clothes. The whole room smelled strongly of marinara sauce.

"*You son of a bitch!*" She whirled on Brent. "Is this your idea of a *joke?* You're *sick*—"

"No, sis," Brent said, holding up a hand as if to ward off a slap. Margot noticed, for the first time, that his hands and clothes were also smeared with the red substance. "I wish it was, I—I don't know what this is."

She looked back at Darren. He hadn't moved. She realized his right hand was gone, as if something had chewed it off at the wrist. This was the source of the red stuff—it pooled thickest around the stump. Only the last two fingers remained on Darren's left hand, with the thumb and most of the palm gone as well. Red ooze there too.

Some kind of suicide? He *had* seemed miserable ever since Hannah left, but she'd never have thought he'd do anything so drastic.

She realized his eyes were open. But there was something wrong with them. They were darker than she remembered. Much darker.

Margot stepped closer, her shoe touching the thick red mess, and bent to examine Darren's face. She noticed the odd lumpy texture of Darren's skin, a thick sheen of oil she'd never seen before. His mouth, too, was smeared with red.

She shivered, made herself look into his eyes.
And met the sightless stare of two huge, black, pitless olives.

he who takes from gwangi

THE CRATER'S CENTER plunged into the earth in a place just northwest of the coastline.

At first, Harry only saw it as a crater. Later he recognized it as more of a valley. It measured more than a hundred miles in diameter and sank about twelve miles below ground level at its deepest. Beyond lie the Gulf of Mexico, and a little farther out, the southern coast of the United States.

The air within it seemed to shimmer, though whether from humidity or some other, more mysterious energy Harry was no longer sure.

This part of the peninsula had been reclaimed by nature, virtually overnight. Many people were just gone, and even some of the buildings had vanished, as though they'd never been there at all. As though the land had never even been cleared. Nothing but new-old growth in their place.

This wasn't what Harry expected when he came to Chicxulub, to spend two months as a visiting physician. He'd expected sun and relaxation, after two grueling years of residency in emergency medicine in Chicago.

He'd been in the coastal village three weeks before it happened. He liked the isolation, and the friendliness of the people. The clinic, though small, was well maintained and supplied, and his paramedic, Mário, was not only intelligent and well trained, but also excellent company. And handsome. The attraction was immediate, and—Harry was certain—mutual.

The remaining people hoped for rescue but expected to be stranded for many days or even weeks before help arrived. Between the two of them, Harry and Mário had secured enough supplies for at least six days, with careful rationing. Harry hoped they'd be prepared to scavenge for more or live off the land if necessary. All their foodstuffs were smoked or canned or in packets. Their watches and compasses still worked, though their phones and computers didn't. Something to do with the thickened trees, perhaps.

On the first day of his second week in Chicxulub, Harry had leaned forward in the little outdoor market and pointed to a pyramid of big drumsticks stacked beside an old woman. The woman flashed a toothy smile as she handed across a sample and carefully pronounced the name for his foreign ear.

Pollosaurio.

Harry took the drumstick, studying it. It was more-or-less like any other chicken drumstick. Just longer, heavier in his palm. The skin had been breaded and fried to an almost red-orange tinge, and it smelled good.

"*Pollosaurio,*" the woman said again. "New. From Chile."

Just then a man jostled past, holding vermilion-combed chickens high as they flapped and squawked outrage on their way to slaughter.

"*Pollosaurio,*" the woman said a third time, pointing to the birds.

Harry touched the man's shoulder and he held the chickens for the gringo to see, challenging Harry to recognize them. Big, but no more so than the average Jersey Giant. Though their legs were unusually long, and their beaks—

Their beaks were not beaks. They were too short. Too round.

Snouts. Almost crocodilian in shape, complete with tiny teeth.

The man might as well have stridden forth from a land lost to time, bearing a bounty from prehistory.

He who takes from Gwangi the evil one is cursed.

The line, from an old Western fantasy film Harry's father loved, popped into his head as he turned the strange, heavy drumstick in his hand.

Pollosaurio.

It shouldn't exist.

A year ago, he supposed, it hadn't.

Suddenly he longed to observe the birds in their natural habitat, perching on low branches or lurking under the leaves of some bush.

He sank his teeth into the *pollosaurio*'s crunchy fried skin.

A burst of flavor coated his tongue. He was back in North Louisiana, offered his first tiny piece of fried gator by a friendly restaurant owner when he was just a little boy. That shell-shocked moment of delicious flavor and texture.

He rolled the meat around in his mouth, eyes closed, tasting the past, imagining the time when creatures like these once flourished, before an asteroid razed the landscape. Under the hammer heat of the tropic sun, surrounded by the cry of dying dino-chickens, he was one with paradise.

He held the bone in his hand, smiling at the resurrection he'd found.

The woman beamed, sure of a sale. From around her neck, a gold crucifix glinted. "*¿Cuánto cuesta?*"

Harry pocketed the *pollosaurio*'s bone. "I'll take a kilo. *Un kilogramo.*"

He handed over a plastic bag without bothering to bargain. Whatever she asked, it would be too little. Miracles were worth the world, after all.

The woman handed across the *pollosaurio* drumsticks, and he almost laughed with pleasure.

I'm hefting a sack of miniature tyrannosaur legs.

In this valley, all things seemed possible.

Rain beat at the pailing roof, roaring down the gutters to splash in a torrent on the ground. From the clinic Harry couldn't make out the beach, let alone the ocean beyond.

Mário emerged to stand next to him on the porch, just out of the rain, extinguishing the glowing tip of his e-cig and carefully tucking the device into a shirt pocket. Nothing but a scarecrow, with stringy muscle on his bones, but still handsome. Amidst the shock and uncertainty, they'd become quite close, living in the clinic the past three days. Or was it four? Everything ran together into an exhausted, terrifying blur.

They were careful exploring their new environment. In the new, invading forest one might encounter jaguars or boa constrictors. One might hear a sudden croak, watch a *pollosaurio* startle from a low branch and, distracted, step on a pit viper. Rumor had it the bogs and streams hid peculiar new reptiles in addition to the resident crocodiles.

Far more unsettling, though, was a low, rumbling growl at dusk. The wind off the sea dulled their ability to gauge its exact direction, but looking inland on clearer days they could see only black water and motionless gray kapok trees. They heard the sound every evening, and every evening it grew louder, closer.

For weapons, the two of them had managed to secure several knives, a couple of old handguns, and one rifle. Violence hadn't yet broken out among the others, but they expected it any moment. Mário kept a daily record in a private waterproof journal. Harry wondered if the Mexican shared the tiny spark of excitement he felt beneath the constant unease.

Harry fished for his own cigarettes—he hadn't smoked since undergrad, but he'd traded his useless phone to a fisherman for half a pack—and lit one. As he smoked, he thought of the *pollosaurios*. The creatures were everywhere, much more numerous and every bit as wild as the region's native turkeys, foraging on the ground for insects and other small animals.

Guess I got my wish.

Other sounds emerged from the rain: that low rumbling, louder than ever before, and frantic shouts in Spanish.

Mário nudged Harry's shoulder, pointed inland.

An enormous, gray-feathered monster moved behind the trees, exerting its presence with a final growling moan before coming into view, striding forward on a pair of massive three-toed feet. The blunt head, more than ten feet above, was naked and red like a turkey vulture's; the long, tufted tail ended some thirty feet behind...

It's not real.

Even at this distance, the tyrannosaur's steel-gray feathers were almost beautiful, shimmering in the rain like the valley air itself. Harry felt the vibration of tons coming down with each claw-footed step, and despite everything his excitement swelled along with his fear.

Mário aimed the rifle in a trembling, white-knuckled grip—Harry hadn't even noticed him retrieve it—and it coughed on his behalf. The tyrannosaur halted, weaving its head about on that short, muscular neck, and roared. A deafening, hollow sound.

Others attacked it, shooting from the sides. The dinosaur turned and moved toward the closest, lunging under the hammer of rain. The gunfire stopped from that side.

Harry stood as though rooted to the ground, frozen with terror, disbelief, and—yes—an undeniable childlike thrill.

Mário cut loose with the rifle again. The monster stood there, swaying a little, and roared again.

It can't be real.

Was it even bleeding? The rain obscured everything.

The tyrannosaur made an about-face, coming right for them with incredible speed. Mário dashed forward, down from the porch, shooting. Harry shouted his name, but Mário didn't stop. All at once, Harry's limbs came to life and he ran to catch him.

The tyrannosaur struck almost as quickly as a snake, and Harry had an instant's glimpse of Mário mid-air, vanished from the chest up. The noise wasn't loud, but he heard it with his whole being. He saw the blood this time.

Harry threw up an arm, skidding in the mud. Instinct and momentum sent him to the ground. He heard the impact of Mário's body less than a meter away, and the tyrannosaur hooting above. Its raised foot filled the sky—

—and came down.

The giant talons squelched in the clay mere inches from Harry's leg before lifting off as the animal rushed at another man. The water that filled the massive footprint was tinged red.

"Mário," Harry croaked. "Mário, Mário."

After silencing two more guns, the tyrannosaur screamed and turned back toward the forest. It staggered back into the trees with a new, marked limp, and the dwindling gunfire ceased.

After an age, Harry got to his feet, trying not to let himself look at what remained of Mário.

Two others were dead, and another severely wounded with a shattered tibia and a broken lumbar vertebra. He'd probably never walk again, if he lived.

The tyrannosaur didn't return, though monstrous sounds continued to haunt them from the trees for days. The attack unified the survivors. Harry no longer feared violence from any of the remaining townsfolk, his position as a doctor more important than ever.

After three hasty burials, he read Mário's notes. They hypothesized that whatever was going on originated with the Chicxulub crater itself. That the crater acted as some sort of portal. *Una puerta de entrada a través del tiempo.* A gateway through time, offering rebirth to those things that had been wiped out as a result of the crater's formation.

A handful of the others claimed the phenomenon stretched as far as Costa Rica, but how could they know? Some still hoped for refuge in Mérida. Many had ventured inland before the attack, deeper into the newly dense forest, hoping to reestablish contact with the capital. None returned.

Harry thought of the *pollosaurios*. They swarmed the valley almost unchecked. Some of the others trapped them for food. Harry refused to partake.

He who takes from Gwangi the evil one is cursed.
Because the cost of miracles is evidently the world.

Or at least, it seemed, the state of Yucatán.

The Chileans had found some new way to disinter the past. Perhaps it worked too well.

in kansas

AS SHE SAT on her desk eating the mosasaur, Hannah reflected on what had taken place in this little office building during the previous three days. Nothing would return to normal. All their lives had moved into a more bizarre, more threatening dimension.

At least now they had food for a little while longer.

***

The morning it started was a nice May morning. What made it nice was fourfold: one, the worst heat wave in West North Central history had broken the night before; two, Hannah had kept her breakfast down; three, the squirrel she spotted on the way to her car.

And four: for the eleventh consecutive night, she hadn't dreamt of Darren.

The heat wave broke under a lash of vicious thunderstorms across northeastern Kansas. Just before dark the previous night, Hannah sat next to the window in the overpriced cell of her studio apartment and watched the first storm beating its way across town toward her. All day the air had been still, the American flag her landlord put up lying limp against its pole, the heat a solid thing. That afternoon Hannah had gone swimming at the public pool, but the water was no relief unless you went in the deep end up to your mouth. Hannah didn't like to go that deep.

At six she'd picked at a cold tzatziki-and-cucumber sandwich and potato salad for supper, a tall glass of Pepsi over ice. Afterwards out back to smoke, fanning herself with one hand and looking across the flat gravel lot of her building to the shuttered grocery store on the far side of the alley. Cars droned back and forth over bone-dry pavement, just out of sight beyond the fence. To the south, dimly flashing thunderheads massed like a barbarian horde.

Back indoors, Hannah tuned her vintage transistor radio to the classical music station and watched the storm approach. The radio brayed static with each lightning flash. She shut it off after it cut to the news—something about a loss of contact with part of Mexico. The heavy rain pattered her to sleep that night. She didn't dream of Darren.

In the morning, after a regrettable amount of veggie bacon and orange juice, she emerged to sunny skies, light wind, and temperatures below ninety for the first time in weeks. On the western horizon, more thunderheads already encroached on the blue.

The first storm had not been kind to the gravel lot. Big round puddles reflected the sky like miniature quarry ponds. At the edge of the farthest, a wary squirrel drank. Hannah watched it for a moment before unlocking her PT Cruiser, sure the sudden noise would scare the rodent off. Watching its cautious sips, she remembered an episode of *Planet Earth* in which Nile crocodiles had ambushed wildebeest crossing the Mara River. The slow-motion shots of the animals thrashing in the brown water, backed by melancholy strings, had felt like a series of Romanticist paintings brought to life.

Comparing the memory to the sight before her now, Hannah couldn't help but chuckle. The puddle was semi-opaque and at least three feet across, but she doubted it concealed anything more sinister than a drowned earthworm or two. She got in the car, turning back to see that the squirrel had indeed bolted, and made the one-mile drive to work with Grieg on PBS. More news of Mexico—still no contact with Yucatán—just before she shut the car off.

The lawn of the Business and Technology Center was flooded right up to the building. Never in Hannah's eighteen months at the BTC had she seen it so saturated. The flowerbeds planted along the concrete foundation were sure to drown. The shallow bowl of the near-empty parking lot was one giant rain puddle, coming nearly to the top of Hannah's shoes as she crossed it.

The storm drains must be clogged.

On her way up to the Ballardon Symphony Orchestra office on the second floor, Hannah stopped at the vending machine for another Pepsi. She could almost hear her teeth and stomach cursing her, but caffeine was necessary, and she hated Bill's coffee.

"Another storm's coming," Bill said, by way of greeting. Thunder boomed, as though to underscore his words. Bill—big, red-faced, fortyish—sat at his desk by the window, watching the sky. He was a music librarian, like Hannah, but he was also the BSO's operations manager, and therefore, technically, her boss. As was often the case, it was just the two of them in the office today. Gerri, the executive director, worked from home most of the time and only came in a few times a month; the rest of the board only met once a quarter.

Through the window, the slow-gathering clouds twisted and rolled, now black, now purple, now veined, now black again. They gradually spread, and by quarter-to-nine Hannah could see a delicate caul of rain extending down from them. It was still some distance away. She slipped a Mussorgsky disc into the big old boombox on her desk, keeping the volume low, and got to work.

At ten Hannah felt nature's call and was glad she'd avoided Bill's coffee. She went out through the office door, with its frosted-glass window straight out of an old *film noir*, and almost bumped right into Doug Elrick's backside.

Doug Elrick worked for a small cybersecurity company located on the first floor, on the opposite end of the building. He was about Hannah's age, in his mid or late twenties, and of average height and build except for what looked like a developing beer gut. He was always unshaven, but evidently incapable of growing a full beard.

Hannah only knew who Elrick was because he'd added her on Facebook last year after several wordless encounters in the hallway. She'd rejected the friend request, not only because he bore a passing resemblance to Darren, but also because she just didn't know the guy or particularly care to.

If he really wants to be my friend, she thought, *he can introduce himself in person.*

Of course, he'd added her again a few months later, still without so much as a "hi" in the hallway or even on Messenger. She'd let it sit unanswered this time, hoping he'd take the hint.

He was walking towards the second-floor bathrooms now, an old Piers Anthony paperback dangling from one hand. Moving slow enough that she'd have to overtake him or look suspicious. He'd done this a couple of times since the second friend request had gone ignored. She could feel his eyes on her as she continued past him and ducked into the ladies' room.

She eased the door shut on its hinges and paused. There were bathrooms on the first floor, much closer to Elrick's office. It was possible they were fully occupied or out of order, but something in Hannah's gut made her doubt it. She took a little longer than she needed to, and when she peeked back into the hall Elrick was nowhere to be seen. She hurried back to the orchestra office on light feet, just in case he might burst from the men's room.

The veil of rain looked much closer through the window. The parking lot looked almost like a shallow lake, with tiny rolling wavelets throwing up spume from the tires of cars. Out in the middle, Hannah could imagine small whitecaps tossing their heads back and forth. It looked deeper than when she'd first come in, even though the new storm hadn't reached it yet.

Watching the water and the approaching sheet of rain was almost hypnotic. The telephone rang, startling her, and as Bill answered it—it was always for Bill—she turned back to the window to see Elrick walking to his rusted ivory Oldsmobile, his sneakered feet sloshing in the now-ankle-deep water.

One of those terrible visions came to her—the kind reserved almost exclusively for anxious young women, she thought—of Elrick withdrawing an AR-15 from his trunk and blowing in her window with a couple of low, hard, coughing shots, sending bullets and glass into Hannah's face, neck, arms...

Such horrors rarely materialized outside the imagination.

But to Hannah's shock, Elrick *did* emerge from the row of cars with something in his hands. Something long and black. Something semi-automatic.

She jerked away from the window, landing hard on both hands.

"What the hell are you doing?" Bill asked, standing from his desk, phone still in hand.

"Get away from the window!"

Bill gave her a startled look, as if he had been awakened from a deep dream. Hannah ran to the wall and hit the light switch, plunging the office into semi-darkness. Bill glanced out the window and started talking rapidly into the phone. After a moment he paused.

"Hello? *Hello?* Are you *there?*"

He hung up, tried to dial out. He hung up again, shaking his head, and pulled his cell phone out of his pocket. "No signal," he said, not looking up from the screen. "You have signal?"

Hannah checked.

"No," she said. "Shit. *Shit!*"

Bill clicked around on his computer. "Internet's down too. *Dammit!*"

The wind whistled outside, high and breathless like the last gasping shriek of a dying thing.

"We need to go downstairs," she said, and realized she was shouting. Trembling.

This is really happening.

Thunder shook the roof and Hannah shrank against the wall.

"Come on!" she yelled. "We have to get out of here!"

Bill nodded and went ahead of her, opening the door to a darkened hallway. The power was out.

Pawing her way along the wall behind Bill, towards the far staircase—the one that led down to the labyrinthine first-floor hallway, itself leading to the side entrance—Hannah thought about the half-ounce of pot in her cabinet at home, untouched for seven months; about the new downtown novelty shop that she kept forgetting to visit; about the photography classes she kept putting off; about the last county fair she'd missed; about Darren with his wrists open or his neck constricted or his head blown off—she'd never known how he'd done it, and never dared to ask, but the casket had been closed...

She had a mighty need for a cigarette.

The first screams sounded from below. Some were cut off by the first gunshots—loud, heart-stopping.

Bill and Hannah froze. She thought of who would be down there at this time: the BTC receptionist, of course, a young black woman about Hannah and Elrick's age; the handful of middle-aged ladies at the hair salon, which would've just opened for the day; the eight or nine teenagers waiting for driving school to begin...

The tears came at once, silent, rushing down her face like raindrops down a windowpane.

The lawyer from across the hall—squat, bald, fiftyish—burst out of his office, along with his assistant, a frumpy middle-aged white woman.

"What the hell is going on?" he cried, voice rising to a weird nasal pitch. "Did you just hear gunshots?"

"Yes," Bill said, adopting a shaky take-charge tone. "There's a shooter in the building. Do your phones or Internet work?"

"No," the lawyer said. "We were just trying to figure it out when we heard—"

Another shot boomed, as though to finish his sentence.

"We should go back to the office," Bill said, as the screams below continued. "Barricade ourselves in. I don't know what we were thinking coming out here." He pulled out his cell. "Still no signal."

"Same here," the lawyer's assistant said, eerily calm. She turned to Hannah. "What about you, dear?"

Hannah didn't answer. She couldn't shake a horrifying sense of responsibility. Perhaps if she'd just accepted his fucking friend request...

No. She almost said it aloud, repeating a version of the mantra she'd perfected after Darren: *You are NOT responsible. This is NOT your fault. Elrick's a psycho. However he's justified this to himself has nothing to do with you.*

But she couldn't make herself move, couldn't make the tears stop.

More gunshots echoed up the stairs.

Hannah forced her hand into her pocket, forced it to grasp the phone and pull it out, forced her eyes down to the screen.

Not a single bar. No Wi-Fi detected.

Somehow, she was certain it was the same for everybody here, for every conduit to the outside world.

"Nobody's coming," Hannah said, wiping her nose. "We have to get out of here."

She took the lead. The old speech pathologist at the end of the hall peeked her head out to look at them as they passed, then slammed her door and locked it. The lawyer stopped to knock, trying to recruit more numbers to their little flock, but hurried to catch up when he saw the group moving downstairs without him.

The four of them made it down the dark spiral staircase, into the narrow, winding hall. Most of the people who worked in the building worked down here. Many were heading in the same direction, toward the side door, using their phones to light the way. They bumped into everything, everyone, each other, in their desperate haste, but few spoke or even made a noise. More than one had blood on their hands, their clothes, their shoes. Some were teenagers.

Hannah kept moving, melding with the larger group and adopting their purposeful silence. From the other side of the building, getting closer, more gunshots. The *click-snap* of a new magazine being loaded, followed by an eerie, melodic whistling. It was a song Hannah had heard countless times, in countless variations: "Over the Rainbow." She had the sense of being herded, but couldn't stop, didn't want to stop.

At last they could see the glass side door, the overcast daylight dimly illuminating the last stretch of hallway.

The floor was wet beneath their feet.

For an instant Hannah was sure it was blood, and she bit back a shriek. Then she looked at the door, and the sheets of water cascading down it, and saw the water running in underneath.

Nobody paused. They all ran for the door. Those in the lead hit it, pushed it open, fell over one another into the shin-deep water beyond. Out in the middle of the lot the tops of cars stuck out like a metal archipelago in the hammering rain, the water almost up to their windows.

How is that possible? Hannah thought. *The lot isn't that deep. It can't be.*

The street beyond was obscured by the heavy downpour, but there seemed to be fewer houses than Hannah remembered…

"Where do you think you're going?"

Hannah turned and saw Elrick standing at the last turn behind them, gun raised. He was smiling, but his eyes were glassy and dead. Wrapped in cellophane and stuck back in his head.

He held the gun ready but didn't fire, didn't move. He seemed to be aiming over Hannah's head, at the people beyond.

The first few were wading out into the storm, up to their knees, now up to their waists. The rest were clogged in the doorway, like one massive being trying to squeeze out. Stuck near the middle, Hannah lost sight of Bill. But she was barely aware of Bill's existence anymore. She just had to get *out*.

Many of the cars were almost buried in the water now, only their tops sticking out. The farthest man, another, taller lawyer who worked on the ground floor, was somehow chest-deep, nearing the center.

The hallway was lit in a series of white-and-purple shutter-flashes. Hannah wasn't sure if it was lightning or muzzle flash, the thunder was so close behind. She heard several people crying as more pushed toward the door, realized she was one of them.

The water's surface churned near the tall lawyer.

He went down.

A heartbeat later he surfaced up to his shoulders, splashing and screaming. He seemed to be having trouble keeping his head above water, even though he should've been able to stand...

He's shot.

Hannah looked back, but Elrick had lowered the gun—it was still pointed at them, but he held it at about stomach-level now. Too low to have hit the tall lawyer from here, though his dead-man's eyes were fixed.

Hannah redoubled her efforts, but more than a third of the crowd had stopped pushing forward. They were watching too.

More people splashed their way into the lot, many of them ignoring the tall lawyer, pursuing their own safety.

Then Hannah saw the blood.

It colored the water around the screaming man, staining his clothes in a perverted baptism as the storm roared. Two seconds later something big splashed in the blood and the tall lawyer went down again. He didn't come up this time.

It was so fast Hannah couldn't be sure she'd seen it at all, really. Just a slim blue-gray hump breaking the surface, with a matching shark's fin some three yards behind. It had vanished in an eyeblink.

All at once the storm lulled to a light drizzle, though the heavy clouds remained. The farthest people, now a few yards beyond where the tall lawyer had gone under, were up to their necks, now swimming for their lives. Hannah found herself closer to the doorway than ever before, within an easy shove or two of freedom...

But as she looked to the far edge of the parking lot, she saw there was no more edge. The street was gone, replaced by water that stretched as far as she could see. Only a loose smattering of houses, trees, and streetlamps remained to mark where it had been. Far fewer than Hannah remembered, and all semi-submerged. She couldn't see her apartment building.

What the fuck?

"Jesus Christ," she heard Bill murmur nearby.

"The whole town is flooded!" someone else cried.

"Where's my *house?*" wept another, further back.

Another pair ventured out into the water as the crowd descended back into babbling, sobbing, and screaming. One or two pushed *back*, as though they'd forgotten about the shooter.

Hannah turned to look at Elrick, glad she'd managed to put most of the crowd between them, but ashamed of that gladness. The gun was frozen at hip-level. The cellophane-wrapped eyes stared disbelieving into what used to be the parking lot.

A smile curled the edge of his mouth.

"*There's something in the water!*" someone screamed.

An Asian woman, maybe Bill's age, wading back to them as fast as she could. She was waist-deep, only six or seven yards out. More were coming back behind her, also screaming about something in the water. Cries of "snake!" and "alligator!" and even "shark!" echoed in the gentle rain.

It was real then. Whatever it was, it *was* out there.

Still, many swam on—Hannah could barely see the farthest bobbing heads anymore.

The Asian woman was now calf-deep, almost to the door.

Lightning and thunder exploded from the hallway. Once, twice, half a dozen times. The woman fell. The nearest swimmers went down, splashing. More blood colored the water.

Hannah whirled amidst renewed screams to see Elrick with gun raised once more, a tiny tendril of smoke twisting from its barrel like a ghost parasite fleeing a dead host.

He grinned.

"Still my show," he said. Hannah could barely hear him over the whimpering group, but she thought his voice trembled.

He's afraid too, Hannah realized.

Of the nearly forty people Hannah knew would've been in the building today, fewer than twenty were clustered in this hallway.

If we rush him, he might only kill one or two more...

She couldn't make herself say it aloud. Couldn't risk leading them to their doom. She looked at the woman sprawled in the shallows, as if to warn herself back into compliance.

"Hannah. Come here."

Hearing Elrick use her name, and with such unearned familiarity, made her skin crawl. She didn't move. She didn't want to give him the satisfaction, to admit defeat with her obedience. More than that, she wasn't sure her legs could work anymore.

But she jumped at a hand on her shoulder, whirling to see it was only Bill. His face frozen in a pained, terrified expression.

"C-come on," he said in an attempt at a comforting tone. "We'd…we'd better do what he says."

Hannah let Bill lead her back to the group. Elrick stood a few steps away, gun ready, barrel swaying from target to target.

"I don't know what the fuck is going on," he said, almost breathless. "But this is still my show. *I'm* in charge." He paused a beat, as if expecting a challenger to step forward. Nobody did. "Okay, then. Let's, uh…let's make a nice, single-file line and go upstairs. Men in front, women in back. I'll be the caboose." He looked at Hannah, the AR's barrel drifting up to point at her eyes. "*You* in the very back, by me." He grinned again, cellophane eyes roving up and down Hannah's body, only resting for a moment on her face. She'd seen Darren make that same leering expression before their breakup, often in partial jest. It had never been a turn-on; seeing Elrick do it now sent a chill of revulsion through her body.

A few people lined up as ordered. Most stayed where they were.

Elrick stepped back, brandishing the gun like a terrorist in a cheesy faux-patriotic film. "Come on!" he shouted. "Line up! Let's go!"

It was almost too dark to see the old woman creep around the corner, scissors in hand. Hannah recognized her as the speech pathologist from upstairs. Elrick had his back to her. She crept closer, scissors raised, like the righteous ghost of Norma Bates. Hannah could almost hear Bernard Herrmann's iconic score building over the image.

The old woman's shoe slapped in the first inches of water, which now, Hannah realized, stretched back almost to the hallway's bend.

Elrick turned at the sound.

The woman lunged with the scissors.

They came together, the gun went off, and they came apart again: the woman with half her throat blown away, Elrick with a large pair of office scissors protruding from his forearm. Hannah thought of Darren, the closed casket…

The wind picked up again. For a heartbeat Elrick stood there, staring at the scissors buried at least an inch in his flesh. The others stood and stared with him.

Now, Hannah thought, still unable to say it aloud, let alone act herself. *Rush him NOW!*

Elrick spun around, firing, as though he'd heard her mental plea. Hannah didn't see how many were hit. She only saw Bill drop to his knees, clutching at the new perforations in his stomach before keeling over to one side. It didn't even look real, like an actor doing a bad death scene.

Now, finally, the crowd converged on Elrick, like the mob on Lon Chaney at the end of *The Phantom of the Opera*. Hannah remembered a screening she'd attended with Darren, with a live orchestra, just like in 1925. It hadn't been as glamorous as she'd hoped—the orchestra was smaller than her high school band class, and they were always a second or two behind or—worse—ahead of the action on the screen.

The gun went off a final time as Elrick went down beneath their screaming, pummeling fury. Even the short second-floor lawyer and his assistant took part.

They would tear him to pieces.

Hannah waded into the fray, found the gun somehow unclaimed in the mass of limbs, and seized it for herself. It was heavier than she expected.

"*Stop!*" Hannah raised the gun for emphasis but didn't dare put her finger on the trigger. She expected them to ignore her, to not even hear her, to continue beating and stomping away until Elrick's brains mingled with the rising water.

But they stopped. They stopped almost as one. Some looked at her as though desperate for guidance, others looked away toward the walls or the lightning as though ashamed or embarrassed.

Elrick was on his back, arms up, trembling. Blood from his nose and mouth matted his sparse beard. One eye was already blackening. The scissors had fallen or been ripped out—blood ran freely from the wound.

The storm was cranking up again, though Hannah wasn't sure it even mattered anymore. The water had risen even in the lightest rain. The cars were no longer visible at all, and in the hallway the water was almost knee deep.

Hannah pointed the gun at Elrick. "Get up, Doug."

Elrick flinched at the sound of his name and looked up at her.

"Get up, I said."

Elrick got up, grimacing. Several of his teeth had been knocked out. Nobody helped or hindered him.

Now Hannah touched the trigger. "Swim."

Elrick's eyes got big, the cellophane gone. Just a little boy's eyes in a young man's beaten face.

They reminded Hannah of Darren's eyes, in some of their last fights.

"What?"

"I want you to swim." Hannah made each word deliberate, raising the gun a little. She stepped out of the way, allowing him a clear path to the parking lot that was.

"Really?"

"Yes." Hannah raised the gun a little more, sighting along the barrel toward Elrick's torso. She couldn't stop her arms from shaking. There'd be no uncertainty this time.

I am sending this man to his death.

"Now. *Swim.*"

"Oh," Elrick said. "Oh, Jesus." His eyes were big and frightened, but he started forward. Nobody pushed him, though someone did offer a half-hearted curse or cheer.

The wind howled. Lightning flashed.

"That thing will get me," Elrick said, pausing, as the thunder followed. He wasn't pleading, just stating a fact. He didn't look at Hannah, didn't take his eyes off the new lake, or sea, or whatever it was now.

"If it does, it does," Hannah said. She realized there was a chance he might survive—at least for a while. For better or worse, the realization steadied her arms. Whatever was out there, it hadn't taken *all* the swimmers. It couldn't have. Unless there was more than one.

"I can't," Elrick said, even as he resumed walking. As though, gun taken away, a few blows landed, he had fallen into a compliant trance. Or perhaps just a defeated one.

He deserves this. He's earned this.

She knew she'd never forgive herself this time. But as she watched Elrick wade out, arms dangling at his sides, she decided it didn't matter. The water lifted him off his feet, and he began to kick and paddle toward the horizon. All the houses were gone now, as well as the trees and streetlamps. All the swimmers too, alive or dead.

Nothing but water.

Hannah had to will away the image of the BTC standing like an isolated island amid a vast sea.

A long, sleek form skimmed the surface, closing on Elrick. A strong, lizard-like tail propelled it toward him with powerful back-and-forth strokes, topped with a triangular shark's fin near the tip.

Hannah didn't hear him scream, even as the pointed snout drove him partway out of the water. Even as the toothy, triangular jaws closed over his head. A monstrous front flipper slapped the surface, almost as loud as the AR. Nearly a third of the thing had breached this time, and it slid forward and down in a belly-flopping motion, dragging Elrick down with it.

It looked like some kind of dinosaur.

There were a few panicked murmurs about time travel and the end of the world. At least one person began praying.

Have *we gone back in time?* Hannah couldn't make herself believe it, despite everything. If anything, she thought, it seemed the distant past had come forward to *them*. To swallow Ballardon, maybe Kansas, maybe the world, almost whole.

Silence fell. For a moment, only the rain had voice. It was getting heavy again.

Hannah went back upstairs, leaving the rest to do what they would, hoping there were some cigarettes left in her purse.

She still held the gun, low and heavy in both hands. There couldn't be many bullets left.

***

She smoked her last cigarette two days later, trying to suppress the emptiness in her stomach.

Shooting the reptile had not been as dramatic or even as difficult as Hannah had expected. Nothing worthy of a thrilling John Williams cue. It was a big target, and swam close to the building often, no doubt hoping for more desperate swimmers. She'd been able to hit it from a broken-out second-floor window as it made a slow pass near the side entrance, just below the surface. The gun emptied fast, and out of the seven or eight shots she took, one right after the other, she wasn't sure any of them had hit until the water calmed and she saw the large, lizard-like body floating on its side, oozing blood. It was over in less than a minute.

The hardest part came after, getting enough people to wade out and help drag it in. Most were still too afraid of the water. But some feared starving even more. And even with Elrick gone, Hannah was convinced the most immediate danger remained within the BTC. With its two floors and twenty offices, its ransacked vending machines and barricaded meeting rooms, useless driving school and flooded salon—all abandoned in this new, shallow sea—the building still offered opportunities for violence.

Her own office was the last place Hannah could still feel a vestige of her former life. Despite all old efforts to detach herself from her three-dozen-odd neighbors—a single baker's dozen now, perhaps the only mammals left in the state—and the trivial disputes and irritations that had until recently provided their only sense of community, it was here she now felt safest. Here, in this office, sitting beside a small fire of phone books by the open window, eating roast hindlimb of *Clidastes* with Stravinsky blaring from her antique boombox.

When she slept, she didn't dream of Darren.

nightbird

*For her house inclineth unto death, and her paths unto the dead. None that go
unto her return again, neither take they hold of the paths of life.*
     -       Proverbs 2:18-19 (KJV)

'Tis here the filthy Harpies form their nests,
Who from the Strophades the Trojans drove,
With sad forebodings of their future Ills.
Their Necks and Visage human are, their Wings
Spread wide, their Feet are arm'd with gripping Claws,
And their swoln Paunches cover'd are with Plumes:
From these dire Trees they utter their complaints.
     -       Dante's *Inferno*, Canto XIII (Rogers)

Part One: A Fool There Was

1

I LOST MY virginity at 6 p.m. on a Friday in the first half of October. The
noise of the ancient bed frame was almost as loud as the owls' screeching
outside. The taker's half-insane housemates were in the room, staring but
never speaking.

She was a pale young woman with a remarkable, mature face. Her
large, green eyes expressed a proud autonomy and nigh-preternatural
intelligence.

Her house was full of great musty books, some centuries old, which
were fast falling to pieces with wormholes and age. It was a home from
which most standards of order, cleanliness, and even modernity had long

since disappeared. She had no computer, television, or telephone of any kind.

Her name, of course, was Lilith.

2

My family lived in a castle in Baraigne County, Illinois. We weren't wealthy, but people thought we were rich because of our home. Purpose and will made it possible; eight or nine years and a little help from his friends was enough for my carpenter father to do wonders. Though the castle was a lonely place at times, it was also marvelous, and I don't think much more money would've significantly added to our comforts.

It stood on a small hill in a forest Dad used to call the Enchanted Wood. The driveway turned aside before its motorized drawbridge (the only working one of its kind in the whole United States, according to Dad) and curled around to the garage in back, like a white gravel python. Its many-windowed front and pseudo-Gothic towers rose over a shallow, algae-green goldfish pond Dad called *"the moat."*

An uneven glade surrounded it, and to one side a wooden bridge crossed a stream that wound in deep shadow through the wood, which extended for acres beyond the property line. The nearest city was Baraigne, nearly fourteen miles south.

***

The castle is where I first took a life.

I was nine years old, armed with a crude homemade walking stick almost as tall as I was, marching into the tree-dotted clearing that was our front yard. The sun was out, but filtered by a thin screen of cloud cover. The air was neither hot nor cold.

I was a knight with a lance, patrolling the castle grounds.

I reached the spot Mom had indicated, and after a few seconds, I saw it: the monster that had invaded our kingdom to terrorize her, the scaled worm I'd come to kill.

A thin brown snake, maybe two feet long at the most. It slithered, slow and silent, along the base of a baby conifer Dad planted a year or two earlier, its body almost hidden in the scattered weeds and pine needles. I watched it move, suddenly unsure—right then, I was a little boy again. The snake was harmless; somehow, that made it more threatening.

Before I could lose my nerve, I struck.

I should've bisected it with a shovel the way Dad always did, or with the rusted machete he kept in the garage. I should've ended it quickly with a swift stab at its head, crushing the tiny skull. But that didn't occur to me. Instead, I beat down at it with heavy overhead swings. With the first strike, it writhed and twisted like an impaled earthworm, stirring the weeds with a rustling sound that was the only noise except for the impacts of my stick and my own heartbeat thudding in my ears. After the first few strikes I wanted it to stop. Nothing was as I thought it might be. I was no saintly hero and this was no draconic beast, no grand battle in an Enchanted Wood. But I couldn't stop, couldn't leave it wounded or crippled. I had to finish what I'd started. My eyes were blurry, my cheeks warm and wet. It took forever to die, and when its throes finally ceased, my arms were tired and my temples throbbed. Tears and snot moistened my lips, sobs wracked my chest.

I went back inside with the knowledge that I'd done something terrible.

When Mom saw me, she hugged me tight.

"I'm sorry," she said. "I'm so sorry. You have such a big heart."

3

In the thick of the forest behind the castle stood a ruined, roofless hut of sticks and plywood, filled with moldering owl pellets and yellow lichen. In my childhood I invented countless legends to explain the spot's desertion, too many and too juvenile to recall. One experience, however, stands out true in my memory.

On a cold, late-October afternoon, the clarity of the light was perfect despite the hunkering gray rain clouds. Withered hawthorn berries dangled on discolored brambles, honey locust pods and hedge apples crunched and slimed underfoot, and the chill of the soaked earth oozed up through the soles of my shoes. The stark trees looked anorexic.

Even at twelve, I had a haunting sense of the imminent cessation of being. The Divorce loomed already, and though it wouldn't be announced for another year, I could feel it coming. Especially in the sickroom hush of the forest that day. In such introspective silences I usually turned to the comforting rage of Judas Priest's *Screaming for Vengeance*, but today I'd left my Discman inside.

I stepped between the first trees and, just like that, the Enchanted Wood swallowed me up. Once inside, you had to stay until it let you out again. Grass had grown over Dad's path years before and now the rabbits and the coyotes made their own runs in the subtle labyrinth, leaving few clues to guide a mere kid. Crows played tag in the branches above, cawing. That little stream had grown sullen with the time of year. It would freeze soon, the mist in the thickets already the color of an old man's beard. Half-stripped branches hung over my head like an endless net.

I walked until the net seemed to break over the hut's dim clearing. It waited for me with the patience of a dead thing.

He stood there, an apparent king of birds and beasts. Ashy doves and diminutive wrens crouched at His feet. On the trunk of an Osage orange tree, a pair of squirrels clung, watching Him. He wore a mask of uncanny whiteness, gleaming like an oval of ice, which turned towards me.

He laid His irrevocable hands upon me. Though I couldn't see them, I imagined His eyes were green. Predatory, carnivorous eyes.

I was afraid of the way His white mask gleamed, the way His huge, ivory-colored hands settled on me like darkness settles in the evening.

I turned and ran. Off came my jacket in His long fingers.

Cold, graveyard air stirred the dark woods. It crisped the hairs on the back of my neck and I was afraid He would seize me, afraid of falling down.

I made it back to the castle before sunset. Mom and Dad emerged from whatever fight they were having long enough to express concern and disappointment at my having lost my coat. I didn't mention the Wood King, the name I'd come to bestow on Him, and I'd never told either of my parents about the hut—it was perhaps the only secret that was all *mine*. Dad insisted on going back to find the jacket and Mom agreed; when it came to me, they could usually put aside differences. Perhaps, in this case, they merely sought a respite from each other.

I didn't want to go back, but with Dad I was safe, or imagined I was. After half an hour of fruitless searching, we stumbled upon the clearing. It was cluttered with dead leaves, all silent, all still, with the cool smell of night coming.

There was no hut. No jacket. No Wood King.

Then the first drops of rain fell, and Dad decided we should head back. Relieved, I followed him home like a faithful dog. Mom would take me to Goodwill for another jacket tomorrow. The cost would come out of my allowance, but it was worth it to put this all behind me.

The wind made a singular, wild, rushing sound. My hands shook.

I never returned to the clearing. After a few days, I began to wonder if I'd imagined the whole thing, and within the year I remembered it more as a dream than an actual event.

Now I know better.

***

Not long thereafter, mere weeks before the Divorce began in a storm of screaming and tears and thrown objects, I read *Treasure Island* and *Captain Blood* and went through a short-lived but passionate pirate kick. One day I ventured back into the Enchanted Wood, for the first time since losing my jacket. I made sure to steer far clear of the path that'd led me to the old hut, entering the trees from the opposite side of the castle. I'd smuggled out a tiny wooden chest from my bedroom filled with useless foreign coins, magic rings from gumball machines, and a splinter of a jousting knight's shattered lance from a long-ago Renaissance Fair. I clutched one of Dad's never-used hunting knives between my teeth until the weight of it in my mouth became too much. At my side, I carried a small shovel and a one-gallon Ziploc bag.

I found a wide, dark honey locust, blackened by a long-ago lightning strike, atop a small bulge in the ground, not quite a hill. I carefully scraped away thorns with the knife until I had a patch of clear bark at eye level, a little bigger than my spread hand. Then I dug the knifepoint into the bark and dragged a diagonal line, then another intersecting the first: *X marks the spot*. I placed the knife in the chest, on top of the other treasures. When I closed the lid, it just fit. I hooked the tiny latch, stuffed the chest in the bag, and sealed it. Again, it *just* fit. I dug a hole about a foot deep at the base of the tree with my shovel, placed my treasure inside, and covered it up, patting it down with the shovel blade and spreading some disturbed moss on top.

Ten minutes later, I had the shovel back in the garage. I fantasized about going back and finding the treasure again in a month or a year. Dad never missed the knife and neither he nor Mom noticed the chest missing from my room. They had more important things to consider, and soon enough so did I. Amid the private investigators and lawyers and judges, the suddenly divided family friends and relatives, my parents seemed to forget they'd ever been in love. And I forgot all about knights and pirates and magic rings. The treasure was buried, and stayed buried.

4

We first met in the crowded lobby of the Big Beverly movie theater on the edge of Baraigne. Mom had allowed me to take my new-used car to the midnight premiere of the latest Batman movie, even though finals week approached. I would soon start my first job as the evening cashier at Berean Bookstore and therefore deserved a fun late night out.

"Hello," I said, attempting connection when I noticed the beautiful girl next to me. She met my gaze, replied with a brief, almost timid smile, and passed me by in a pungent swirl of spicy vanilla perfume. I turned around and watched her walk across the theater lobby and out through the glass door. She was a Greek goddess, straight out of *Jason and the Argonauts*. Out on the sidewalk an early summer breeze lifted her long red hair for a moment. And then she was gone.

I needed to know her, to introduce myself. Even as I laughed at the absurdity of the thought, I found myself hurrying across the lobby and out through the door as she reached the end of the block.

As I stood and watched her disappear around the corner, I considered abandoning the movie, running after her. I'd already given up my spot in line... But what then? Besides, I'd looked forward to the Caped Crusader's exploits all year. I went back inside and rejoined the line, which now threatened to spill outside anyway. But I caught myself thinking of her even after the previews.

***

The second Thursday that October, I was about to go on break when she came into the bookstore and stood just on the other side of the counter from me, dressed in white, again fragrant with perfume.

My breath caught. I'd never experienced anything like it. It was a kind of panic, like claustrophobia, yet heavy with erotic compulsion. As I stood there breathless, I stiffened in my khakis.

I glanced sideways, first at her hip, just visible beyond the counter, then at her face. She was looking straight ahead at the Bible embossing machine behind me. Classic, straight nose; large, green eyes, somewhat slanted, seeming lit from within; and wide, full lips glossed with crimson. She moved against the counter and I noticed her waist and the full sway of her breasts. Her dress, though loose, touched her in a way that revealed the luxuriant body underneath.

She's naked under there, or practically naked. She's too sexy to be true.

What could I say to her? Should I say anything? *Could* I?

She trained her pale-green eyes full on me and smiled.

"Hello," she said in a smoky voice.

"Hello." I flushed and grinned, barely recognizing my tone. "How are you?"

"Quite well, thank you." Her intonation made it sound like an altogether different kind of thanks.

"How may I serve you?" Noting her look, I fell back on my customer service routine. "I mean, are you looking for anything in particular?"

"Nothing I haven't already found."

"Okay. Well, uh, let me know if you need anything." I wished my words didn't sound so tight and high-pitched.

She kept her eyes on me. My heart beat five times before she spoke again.

"You desire me," she said.

I didn't reply, but uncomfortably stood back from the counter. My mouth opened and closed again.

She turned away, walking to the door. "Go on break."

She waited for me by the driver's side door.

How did she know which car was mine?

I chalked it up to a lucky guess as I walked over to meet her. The employees-only lot was fairly deserted and how likely was it that a teenage boy drove a minivan?

Without hesitation, she leaned forward and laid her open hand directly between my legs. No girl had ever touched me like that. She was very close now, the scent of her spicy perfume strong. Her lips were parted to reveal the tips of her front teeth. Even her breath smelled of vanilla, warm and soft.

"You desire me," she repeated.

She gave me one quick, hard squeeze, and stood back. Silent triumph filled her expression. I felt a mixture of excitement, embarrassment, and disbelief. Had she actually just squeezed me there, this woman in the white dress for whom every boy in my high school would kill just to sit with?

I grew bolder. "I don't even know your name."

"Lilith."

"Is that all, just Lilith?"

"It's all I need." She smiled.

"I'm Isaac. Could I, um, buy you some dinner?"

"Is that necessary?"

I took three long heartbeats to reply. "Necessary how?"

"You feel it necessary to court me somehow. To buy me dinner, to impress me with your taste in fast food, to make witty small talk. To tell me all those humorous anecdotes that I'm sure your friends and coworkers have heard a hundred times. Is all that necessary?"

I licked my lips. "I guess not."

Her smile widened. "Good."

She extended a hand and plucked a single hair from the shoulder of my black polo, then leaned forward and kissed me briefly, almost shyly, on the lips.

My skin burned, my heart raced. It was like nothing I'd ever felt. And as quickly as she'd made contact, she withdrew. She walked away, without a single backward glance.

After she disappeared around the corner to the customer parking lot, I noticed a square of cardstock left on my windshield beneath one of the wiper blades. It was an old business card for the local hookah lounge and, on the back, a country address written in green ink with a message above it:

> *I hope you'll meet me tomorrow night.*
> *- Your Lilith*

***

Back then, when a traveler in east central Illinois took a certain narrow road in the country on the edge of Baraigne County, he'd come upon a lonely and curious gray-white Victorian clapboard house. As I parked and got out, I wondered if I was at the right place. The white oak trees surrounding it seemed too large, and the wild weeds, brambles, and grasses grew altogether unchecked. At the same time, the planted fields around the property appeared few and barren, while the house in question wore an aspect of age and squalor. A small paddock and stable on the far side of the gravel driveway, though large enough to keep at least three horses, bore only a solitary old Clydesdale. An anemic-looking specimen, with odd sores—something like insect bites—discernible just under the base of his throat.

As I drew near the overgrown walkway, I passed through a stretch of unpleasant mist. Large, sluggish screech owls swarmed the short dirt path in the near dusk. The house had a faint, malignant odor of mold and decay. I hardly remember entering. One moment I was climbing the rickety porch and knocking on the door, the next Lilith was welcoming me in and rushing me through the sparsely furnished common areas to the stairwell. Apart from some houseplants, there were few decorations: a handful of lean, spare, charcoal drawings of naked men and women on the walls, most of them faceless.

Half a dozen roommates filled her house. I might've thought they were family, except they looked nothing like her or each other. The youngest, a thin woman with blond hair cut close to her scalp, had to be about Lilith's age, perhaps a bit older. The oldest, a tall, strong-faced man with curly salt-and-pepper hair, had a look of diminished power and grace not unlike the

Clydesdale outside. His thin, high-bridged nose, dark eyes, and lofty forehead reminded me a little of Christopher Lee. Lilith never introduced me to any of them, and those I met on our way to her bedroom kept to themselves beyond a knowing, jealous glance or two.

It took me years to understand that jealousy.

The September heat had lingered around Baraigne that day. In Lilith's house all the windows were closed. The only sounds in her bedroom were the hum of an ancient air conditioner and a pair of small oscillating fans. Incense sticks simmered and black candles burned, filling the air with a vague, musky odor.

She looked into my eyes.

Tall, beautiful, dressed in white. She watched me, the sixteen-year-old bookstore cashier, with eyes unblinking. Her pale breasts bulged a little from her blouse as she leaned toward me—

(*no bra*)

—came closer, pressed against me. With her small, thin fingers, she touched my hand.

I should've drawn it back, but didn't. Embarrassed, I averted my gaze. Lilith was at least two years my senior and her charms were too savory to resist. Indeed, she'd nullified the attractions of younger, more wholesome girls. I imagined she dabbled in witchcraft, a fantasy delicious for its transgressiveness.

I liked her, even as I disliked the owls outside. Their screeching penetrated the window glass. It would be dark soon and the drive along the countryside was unpleasant by night. Still, I reached between her thighs, beneath her skirt. Her attention filled me with a curious potency, though I was not the master here.

I flushed and withdrew my hand.

She grabbed it.

"Stay awhile. There's thick fog on the road. Besides, I have a good red wine for you."

She stepped back, removed the cork from a dark bottle on her nightstand, and poured its contents into a large glass cup. An odor of hot, delicious spices bloomed, overpowering the less agreeable scents of the incense and candles.

She offered me the cup, and I paused. I'd never had more to drink than an occasional sip from Dad's beer can, though many of my classmates drank, and often. She held the cup closer. "It's wine. It'll warm your stomach...and..." She added something inaudible as I took it.

I inhaled its fumes with some caution but the pleasant smell reassured me. As if warned by some premonition, I hesitated. Then I remembered what it meant to be here, in Lilith's house—in her bedroom. The wine would fortify me for what was to come and one glass wouldn't prevent me from making the dismal return drive to the castle. I drank it quickly and set the cup down on her dresser.

"It's good."

Even as I spoke, I felt in my stomach and veins the spreading warmth of the alcohol, and of something more eager. My blood seethed and thundered in my ears.

For an instant, I was afraid and wanted to flee. My gaze returned to Lilith.

Her skirt and blouse lay at her feet. She stood naked as her namesake. Her limbs and body were voluptuous. Her lips enticed me with a promise of ampler kisses than any other mouth. The convex of her breasts, the roundness of hips and thighs, even the pits of her arms were all fraught with luxurious allure.

She pressed herself against me. "Do you like me, little one?"

This time I met her with hot, questing hands. Her limbs were cool. Her breasts firm but soft. Her body was white and almost hairless, but the gentle roughness of her pubic hair only sharpened my desire. The door opened and her housemates edged into the room along the walls, but I paid them no mind. I was with *her*.

My fingers clawed her back, cupped her breasts. My blood filled with a reckless ardor for which the wine could only claim partial credit.

She caressed me and led me to her bed. It creaked under our naked bodies as the housemates watched.

***

Two needles pierced my chest and I woke with a cry. Dawn hadn't yet arrived, though the black candles had burned down into their sockets. The housemates were gone. Nauseated and confused, I struggled to remember where I was or what I'd done. I turned my head.

An impossible thing knelt on the bed beside me: a large, droopy hag with a pale, warty body sparsely covered in gray-blue hair, except for the long red tangle sprouting from the scalp. Its legs were like those of a massive bird of prey, with huge, sharp talons. From the shoulders, just behind and below the arms, grew a pair of enormous feathered wings the same color as the body hair. Thick, webbed fingers, like those of a fetus, clenched and unclenched with a slow, trancelike rhythm. The horrible round eyes were open, but vacant. From its slackened mouth snaked a long, forked tongue, the prongs of which were embedded deep in the right side of my chest. The creature pressed and bulged against me, twitching in unison with the mad piping of the owls outside, and I felt the rounded softness of something that resembled a breast. The scent of vanilla was almost overpowering.

My limbs and body were heavy. With prodigious effort, I drew myself away from the crushing nightmare shape. It did not stir or appear to waken from its trance and the tongue's prongs withdrew at the least resistance. No change came over the face of the bent thing, or the yellow-green eyes with their great black pupils. The shrilling of the screech owls ceased as I slid from the bed.

Compelled by morbid fascination, I turned back to peer at the thing on the bed—and saw only the gorgeous nude form of Lilith, still asleep. Perhaps the monster had been a false impression, a half-dream that lingered after slumber. I lost something of my horror, remembering the beauty to which I'd yielded. But it was already much later than I'd meant to stay and it was a half-hour drive home.

I left the house, triggering a bright security light over the porch. None of the roommates were out. It was minutes before dawn and a warm mist lay everywhere, shrouding the yard and hanging like a curtain on the path to my car. Moving and seething, the mist seemed to reach toward me with intercepting fingers. I shivered at its touch and bowed my head, drawing my arms close around me.

Though I was not altogether sure of my surroundings, I thought I'd covered half the distance to my car. Then, all at once, the owls emerged. They were hidden by the mist till I came close. Big and bloated, they squatted in my way on the little footpath, hopping before me from the pallid gloom on either side. Several strutted around my feet with a horrible, heavy gait. I tripped over one of them and barely saved myself from a headlong fall on the dirt path.

The yard was alive with owls. They flopped against me from the mist, striking my legs, my chest, my face with their feathered bodies. Dozens of them. I staggered back and forth, tripping, shielding my face with lifted hands. They covered the ground, and their hurtling bodies filled the air, overwhelming me. I knew I'd feel talons in my flesh any moment.

Like the lifting of a dense curtain, the mist rolled away. In the clarity of early sunrise, the house loomed before me. The owls had turned me around, but dispersed in the light of day, scores of them flying back to the trees. Helpless fright and panic gripped me. I was back in Lilith's clutches.

Lilith—naked, beautiful—emerged from the house and came toward me. A sudden gust of wind arose from nowhere, lifting the tangled waves of her long red hair about her head.

"Why did you leave so hastily, little one?" An amorous coaxing in her tone. "You should come back in for another cup of wine."

She came very close to me as she spoke and brushed my lips with her own. Again, the scent of vanilla. Overcome with dizziness, I turned my head away. The simple movement required immense effort, but my mind was clear, and the sick revulsion of that predawn nightmare returned. I saw again the great bird-thing that had knelt at my side.

"I don't want more wine. Let me go."

"Do I frighten you, love? Do you loathe me now? You loved me last night. I can give you all that other women have, and more."

"You're not a woman. You're a—something else. I'd rather... I need to go. Please, just let me go, let me go!" My voice cracked with panic. "Let me go! I need to go!"

The thin smirk slid from her face, leaving it blankly inhuman.

"Go then," she said. The weird paralysis lifted from my muscles. Without a parting word or glance, I turned and ran to my car.

I'd driven little more than half a mile when the fog returned. It coiled toward me in vast volumes from the fields, pouring like smoke onto the road before me. The rising sun softened to an ashy silver disk and disappeared. The sky was lost in a pale, seething void.

Like a mass of clutching arms, the mist drew closer and seemed to enter the car, though the windows were up. Fog thickened in my nostrils and throat, dampened my clothes. I choked with the fetor of rank feathers and a putrescent stench as of half-digested corpses. I thought I saw the outline of a monstrous form sliding across the road, large and heavy and vaguely humanoid, but also somehow birdlike—and behind it something else, something taller and thinner that blended with the mist.

Then the blank whiteness thinned and I was almost home.

I'd examined my chest, where I'd felt the puncture of that forked tongue, discovering only a faint pair of small, red sores, like a spider bite. That's what it must have been—a spider bite. I must have been dreaming or tipsy from the wine. I was doubly comforted, for the woman herself was *not* a dream. Neither was what we'd done—what *I'd* done at last, after years of adolescent desire.

I had relief from virginity.

The first time I wanted to talk about it, Dad and I were sitting in silence on a plastic bench under the trees. The sun was setting behind the trees in melancholy splendor. The creek wound through, almost at our feet, reflecting in its current the fading crimson of the sky. It was a soft, clear evening. Low over the ground a thin film of mist stole like smoke.

"I've got into one of my moping moods tonight," Dad said after a while, and started singing aloud "(I Know) I'm Losing You," the Rare Earth version. During The Divorce he'd often played it on the castle's impressive stereo system, until it was practically his theme song.

I decided not to tell him.

Rite of passage though it was, even my closest friends at school knew nothing of it for weeks until my furtiveness gave way to pride. Although I left out some of the darker, weirder details.

I thought I'd never forget that night, any of it. But over time those weirder details faded from even my memory, though the more enjoyable ones furnished my dreams for years to come.

The first came Halloween night. Lilith appeared naked to me in my room. She pushed me down on the bed, undressed me in soft light, and left me to wake with a painful erection. In later dreams, she kissed me, stroked me, even leapt on top of me, but it always ended before the consummate act.

In one or two of them, I imagined a tall, white-masked figure lurking in the shadows. But in none of them appeared the fat, clawed *thing* that had left its mark on my chest.

Lilith never returned to the bookstore. But I went back to her house before Thanksgiving. Even now, I'm not sure what I expected. Whatever it was, it wasn't a deserted house.

The driveway was vacant, the horse paddock empty. Only a few owls remained, still sleeping in the trees.

Padlocks guarded the front and back doors. I walked around the outside of the house, peeking into the lower windows where the blinds were cracked, but the house was dark and quiet.

After a few minutes, I was certain nobody lived there anymore. The realization filled me with an uneven mixture of dread, relief, and disappointment.

I went home wondering where she'd gone, and hoping I might never find out.

I went back to the house again before Christmas. And again, the month after that. Though the house was always locked and evidently deserted, I took an odd comfort in going there every month, and it soon became a kind of ritual. I needed to check, to see if she would be there *this* time. I don't know if I wanted to see her or not.

But I had to go.

Part Two: The Years We Waste

5

Elizabeth D'Arcy and I had circled each other almost all our lives. We grew up going to the same school, the same church, the same bookstores, and restaurants, and hometown football games, without ever meeting. We were aware of each other, in a nebulous sort of way, but we didn't *notice* each other until the first day of our second semester at Baraigne Community College. By then I was living primarily with my mother in town, while Elizabeth had moved with her parents a year or so earlier to be closer to her grandfather in Foxton, a small town about twenty miles north.

That day in the study lounge I recognized her in a sea of new faces and decided on a whim to sit at her table. We made awkward small talk and I realized for the first time how attractive she was; intelligent, slightly tired brown eyes behind a pair of cute, red-rimmed reading glasses, straight brown hair almost hiding her neck. A full bottom lip that made her look a little pouty and protruded a bit when she smiled. I'm still not sure what she saw in me. Throughout college I was tall, thin, with long, sinewy arms and a brow overgrown with a mop of thick blond hair.

We were in one of the common lounge/study areas on campus, and once I'd decided I was comfortable enough to stay, I took out my laptop— more to temper my rapidly developing crush than to really use it. When I plugged it in, flames spurted from the outlet—actual flames, nearly a foot high! Elizabeth and I screamed, and I yanked the laptop cord out. The flames receded, vanished, and I was left with a scorched but still functional power cord. That, and a nice little memory that I like to think makes a great story—but maybe you had to have been there. Once we were sure the campus wasn't going to burn down, Elizabeth and I collapsed in relieved laughter and minutes later we exchanged phone numbers.

Later, we thought of that moment as the first real spark of romance between us. No pun intended.

The next evening, I took her to Steak n' Shake for dinner and it was as if the small rapport we'd kindled with a burst of electrical fire had never existed. We ate in silence, barely even looking at each other, the nerve to talk lost outside the confines of community college. But she kissed me in the car when I took her home, with Quiet Riot's "Metal Health" on the radio.

***

The car was where we had our first movie date: a double feature on my laptop in the campus parking lot, Fritz Lang's *M* and Tod Browning's *Freaks*. Later we'd graduate to more recent fare at the Big Beverly, mostly action and horror films. We both preferred the older stuff.

The car was also where we first made love— after three weeks of long, almost nightly phone conversations interspersed with lunch, dinner, and movie dates—on a deserted stretch of country road I'd discovered during short-lived flings the previous two summers. Those flings had been fine, but with no fireworks at the end. This time there were fireworks, for both of us, though more than once we had to duck down behind the front seats whenever a pair of passing headlights caught us through the windshield. Each time the headlights slowed as they passed—curious drivers *always* wanted to sneak a peek—and we'd squirm down as low as we could, hoping it wasn't a cop. But pass they did, and eventually we got dressed and were on our own way.

I couldn't help but notice the short, orderly scars on her forearms and abdomen, but I didn't dare ask her about them.

Later we'd park in deserted country cemeteries, more heavily wooded roads, and once even in the long driveway of the castle when no one was home. We rarely used the same place twice.

I thought about taking her to the old Victorian house. I was certain I was the place's only regular visitor anymore, but I found I wanted to keep it that way. Even to give the notion of bringing someone else—especially this girl to whom I'd grown so attached—serious consideration seemed wrong, a violation of some unspoken pact. Furthermore, I'd come to think of the place as partially *mine*. After two years, it was difficult to imagine not being there alone. It was one thing I couldn't share.

***

She told me she loved me five months later. We were seeing a movie—not the latest superhero flick at the Big Beverly, but a psychedelic Japanese horror film from the 1970s at the little old Art Theater downtown. It was about a group of schoolgirls who travel to a creaky country house and, one by one, get devoured by the ghostly place. I'd decided I was in love with Elizabeth some two months before, but when I'd started to tell her she'd stopped me.

"I know," she'd said, putting a finger to my lips. "But don't yet. It's too soon and I want to be sure when I say it back."

Now, sitting in the darkened old theater with my arm around her, smelling her hair, watching this hallucinatory spectacle that was right up our mutual alley, I felt the urge to say it again. I leaned closer and whispered in her ear.

"I—" I began, and stopped, suddenly remembering her words. I kissed her head instead, hoping she hadn't heard—

"What?" she said.

"Never mind," I said. "Nothing."

She looked at me, her dark eyes serious in the movie-screen light. I looked back, suddenly unable to speak. She touched my hand.

"I love you," she said.

"I love you too," I said, and kissed her.

She kissed back.

We never did find out what happened to the last Japanese schoolgirl.

After the movie, out in the country, she confided to me that she'd suffered from depression since junior high or thereabouts, and that she'd stopped taking her antidepressants a few weeks before. She said the pills made her hallucinate, gave her bad dreams. I worried, of course, but nothing I said could change her mind. I'd already guessed as much about her condition from the scars, but was too afraid of losing her to broach the subject.

The next day I entered the old house for the first time since I was sixteen. By then it was decrepit, with one side almost caving in. Even the owls had gone at last. Padlocks remained on the doors, but a couple of hard kicks freed it from the already-cracked frame.

In my final year of high school, I'd tried to collect all possible data on Lilith. I'd been in communication with college professors and visited the campus library. A close survey of *Gilgamesh*, the Babylonian *Talmud*, and the Arslan Tash amulets had supplied terrible clues to her nature, methods, and desires, but talks with several students of archaic lore in town—and correspondence with many others elsewhere—had made it difficult to determine what was true, what was legend, and what was outright conjecture or manipulation. And was any of it *my* Lilith?

But by now there was no more doubting my own experience. My dreams of her had remained an almost weekly experience and they'd only gotten more frightening: huge, brown owls with bloodstained feathers, moving through a choking fog. And always, walking among them, the woman. And something else.

I went through the whole house, visiting all the rooms I hadn't seen before. The huge old kitchen was empty but for a few pots and bowls, and some stale spices left in the cabinets. Something mold-eaten that might've once been a tomato reigned as the sole occupant of the long-darkened fridge. Tattered scraps from old magazines and books littered the floor in a few places, but there were no houseplants, no wall hangings.

Only Lilith's room still had a bed, though it was bereft of pillows or sheets. I gathered up the most complete books in the house and brought them into the bedroom, making a disordered pile on the bare mattress. All were hardbound, and none was fully intact: old editions of Ovid, Dante, Milton, Goethe, Haggard, and Lovecraft.

I sat in that room reading until I saw the sun begin to set through the cracked window. At last, weary, I put the books down and went to that window. There was a single burnt-out candle on the sill, that familiar black wax. I caught sight of my reflection in the fractured glass. I looked haggard myself. I realized at once how terrified I'd been coming here, not just another trip to the house, but *inside*, back to the very room where…

Where *it* had happened.

How foolish that fear now seemed. There was no longer anything here that could hurt me.

I took the least fragmentary book—a torn, somewhat water-damaged first edition of *The Outsider and Others*—and drove home.

On the way, I listened to Queen's "My Melancholy Blues" on tape.

Elizabeth's favorite song.

I didn't bother returning to the house the next month, or the month after that.

6

Over the next two years, Elizabeth spoke occasionally, but with increasing frequency—as well as a chilling, matter-of-fact certainty—about ending her life. New marks had appeared on her abdomen, her lower thighs, the undersides of her arms.

It almost ended things between us. Every time she undressed, I found myself glancing over her in a way I hadn't before. Not admiringly with the eyes of a lover, but with dread. The dread that I'd see a new little red line, applied sometime that day with a sterilized safety pin or thumbtack. More often than not, I didn't. But the old lines were still there, faint against her pale skin, and I knew there would only be more. How long until she traded the safety pin for a pair of scissors or a steak knife or a razorblade? What if she already had?

I knew she could sense me checking her over, and that she felt worse for worrying me so, but I couldn't help it. More than once we'd been about to make love and my exploring hand had brushed a recent cut in her side or on her thigh. She'd winced, I'd borne the lingering stickiness of the wound, and it had destroyed the moment. Every time she took longer than a quarter-hour to respond to a text, I wondered if she might be dead. I couldn't take it.

I pleaded with her to seek some kind of treatment. She insisted that the medication hadn't helped and that therapy would be a waste of time. I reminded her that she'd only ever been on one medication, that she couldn't know if the therapy would be a waste unless she tried it, but she was adamant. I wanted to call someone, tell them—her parents, her friends, anyone who might be able to help—but she said with cold finality that she'd never trust me again if I did.

So I didn't.

But I couldn't go on with her much further, couldn't share a home or a lifetime with her, unless she pursued some kind of help.

Upon transferring out of community college, Elizabeth suggested we move in together within the year. *Before* graduation, earlier than I'd ever envisioned. After some thought, I agreed, but on the firm condition that she either resume her medication or start seeing a regular therapist. I gave her this ultimatum in the car, half expecting her to break down or blow up right there in the passenger's seat. But there were no tears and no shouting matches. She agreed to start seeing a therapist twice a month and, after she'd made her first appointment, we started looking for a place and found one within a few weeks; a small one-bedroom just off campus.

While packing for the move, I rediscovered that old, waterlogged copy of *The Outsider and Others*. I'd kept it on my bookshelf as a sort of trophy after leaving Lilith's house for the last time, but I hadn't thought much about it since. I took a break from packing that evening and leafed through the book, as much as I could. Only a handful of stories in the tome were intact, the rest either were missing pages or rendered partially illegible by time, moisture, or long-dead silverfish.

Several of the stories had notes scribbled in the margins and all of these seemed to have something to do with houses: "The Picture in the House," "The Shunned House," "The Dreams in the Witch-House," and "The Thing on the Doorstep." The oldest-looking notes were in another language—a quick online check confirmed it as German—with English translations below, in another hand. The first line, in clear block letters, read:

RITUAL OF INVOKING

What followed were clearly instructions. Some were smudged, but after the first page it became clear that I had stumbled upon a method of summoning something. And after the second page, the name *Lilith* appeared more than a dozen times in all.

My heart pounded, my legs turned to water with the realization that, in all my fruitless visits to that old abandoned house, the key to calling her back had been right under my nose.

I shut the book, threw it hard across the room. It would have to be destroyed or at least locked away. I hadn't been back to that house in almost three years and I had no intention of rekindling an old obsession.

Of course, my intentions couldn't have been less significant. That night, and most nights after, the memories and the dreams *had* returned.

She had returned.

7

In the living room of our little apartment, Elizabeth stood on tiptoe to kiss me. Baby, our miniature spaniel—actually Elizabeth's, before we'd moved in together—wagged her approval from the sofa. It started as a simple celebratory kiss, congratulating me on securing a paid internship at the university press, but it soon became something more. Elizabeth drew back her head and looked into my eyes.

"Are you trying to start something?" she said, a little breathless.

"Damn right," I said, taking her in my arms.

I pulled her close, her skin warm through the thin material of her summer dress. I kissed her neck where the brown hair curled forward below her ear. We moved closer to the sofa and with one eye I caught my reflection—distorted, fragmented—skating across the black television screen.

Near the end I thought for a moment about Elizabeth, but I knew I was only being dutiful. For months, memories of Lilith had assaulted me with her scent, her texture, her taste. I remembered so well the beautiful face of that red-haired woman in her white skirt, as she stood in that old bedroom, with my clumsy fingers fumbling about her, and the candlelight giving it all a shadowy atmosphere. She knelt over me, put her mouth on me, put me inside her. It was all so quiet that every quavering breath, soft little moan, or creak of the bed seemed loud. I've already forgotten much of my life preceding that event and for certain stretches after it's also obscure, but that scene stands out vivid as an isolated picture surrounded by darkness.

***

I hid *The Outsider and Others* in a shoebox, on the uppermost shelf of our apartment's cramped coat closet. I examined the notes inside almost every chance I got, sneaking peaks when Elizabeth was out, like a kid looking at porn. Studying the invoking ritual in secret became a ritual unto itself, much as visiting Lilith's farmhouse had been. The incantation was longer and more complicated than the Lutheran invocation I'd memorized in church, but before long, I could recite it from memory just as well.

I often thought of destroying the book. One day, when Elizabeth was in class, I took it to the park with the intent of burning it on one of the little public grills. I even brought a small bag of charcoal and a package of hotdogs to avoid suspicion, but I couldn't go through with it.

I didn't want to use the ritual—at least, not then—but I couldn't throw it away either. After all, wasn't this just what I'd been hoping for, just why I'd gone back to that farmhouse so many times? Destroying it would be like deleting all of an ex-girlfriend's contact information; cathartic, perhaps, but with potential for regret. I didn't have to *use* it, but there'd be no harm in preserving it. Just in case.

In fact, wouldn't using it be even more cathartic than destroying it? Perhaps at last I could have some closure. Perhaps at last I could see Lilith for real, even talk to her, for the first time since I was sixteen. Perhaps…

The book remained in its shoebox on the shelf.

8

I went into the bedroom, closed the door behind me, and stood for a long time in the middle of the creaky hardwood floor, thinking. Then I took off my coat and checked my pulse. It was too fast and I felt a little feverish. I'd been preparing for days.

I went to the window. The bedroom overlooked the country road, thin and pale in the distance. No cars rumbled over it. I scrutinized my reflection in the glass. There were tears in my eyes.

I lowered the blinds, but left them open to watch the sunset while I lit the candles I'd arranged in a rough circle throughout the room. My stomach grumbled, but I paid it no mind. The thought of eating before tonight's events had filled me with unease.

At full dark, I closed the blinds.

Once in a while, I flirted with other women on campus and I'd even kissed one after too many drinks at a party. I wasn't proud of it, but it had happened. Several times I'd fantasized about taking things further, especially before the move, but I'd never gotten up the nerve. I'd sure as hell never done anything like *this*.

This is wrong, I thought as I kicked off my shoes. *I'm cheating on the woman I love, the woman who's waiting for me to come home.*

I took off my clothes, went into the special corner I'd prepared, and caressed myself as I spoke the necessary words, more out of eagerness to have the seed spilled and so be unable to change my mind than for the pleasure of it.

My knees buckled with the joyless orgasm. Pain flared as I hit the floor, washed away by expectant trepidation.

I rolled onto my back and waited.

Two heartbeats, three, four.

Then I heard the wings—a steady, somber flapping. My stomach churned at the sound.

I looked up. For a breath, I supposed the noise to be coming from somewhere outside—but I soon dismissed that notion. No ordinary nightbird.

No. The sound was coming from somewhere much more distant. A world far from the room in which I sat.

Far, yet near.

The thought made my breath quick. I'd so anticipated this moment, planned with every wit I possessed. In moments *she* would be here, summoned from wherever she'd settled to bring her ageless head back into *my* world.

I'd worked hard that day to prepare the area for her. The hardwood had been scrubbed and strewn with dark petals. I'd set up a kind of altar to her in the corner—a full-length mirror upon which I'd scrawled numerous phrases and sigils with one of Elizabeth's discarded lipstick tubes, along with an unopened bottle of expensive red wine, all upon a black satin cloth—with a sterile knife and small cup on the left side should she require some spontaneous blood sacrifice. On the right, a plate bearing a dead pigeon.

Not even as a young confirmand, eager for the Rite, had I been so diligent.

But now, as the sound of the wings grew louder, drowning out all else, I was afraid.

"Too late," I murmured, hoping to quell my rising fear. The final task—the spilling of seed—had been performed. The time for hesitation had passed, and regret was pointless.

The doorway is open.

I sat up. My limbs tingled. My head, wrist, and bladder ached.

The candles dimmed and brightened, taking on the rhythm of the wings, burning hottest on each beat. Between beats, the darkness in the room became almost utter. In one beat I saw the writing on the mirror melt away. In the next, I saw the place beyond the room from which the wings flapped. A world of owls, was it? Huge, dark owls on a dusty desert mesa…?

And then, in the final beat, the mirror was just a mirror again. The candles flickered out and I stood in the dark, saying nothing.

And then, light.

It came from *her*, from the creature who now, with the mirror sealed behind her, occupied the room. A cold sort of bioluminescence, the glow of a deep-dwelling thing that never sees the sun. It struck me that I'd never once wondered how she would appear.

Why then was I so distressed to set eyes upon her? There was little here I hadn't already glimpsed as a teenager: the feathery blue-gray hair that covered every inch of her fleshy body, the dusty wings at her shoulders, the piercing talons at her feet. The sickly sweet smell of vanilla she brought with her was so familiar as to be almost reassuring. But I found nothing reassuring or even human in her face. Only an appetite that made my bowels ache.

There was rot on her webbed fingers, and her tongue—twin barbs twitching—dangled between parted lips, almost down to her thighs, as if awaiting a body into which it could plunge. Could I have any doubt that she intended to dispatch me with a penetrating kiss as she had God only knew how many others?

I'd made a mistake, summoning her here. A terrible mistake.

The barbed tongue withdrew as she spoke. "So, you've not finished with me after all," she said in a nearly genderless voice, perusing me as I stood panting on the bare boards. She spoke as if I'd left her mere hours or days ago, rather than years. "Good. Now we shall begin again."

I made no reply. The tongue flicked out like a snake's. "Do you even know who I am?" For an instant her voice was light and breathy, like that of an excited teenager.

"Yes," I said. "I know."

And yet, I'd expected something different. I'd thought she would come as the woman, at least; her thighs ready to spread, her ass firm and weighty, the way I remembered. I'd expected a beautiful body prepared for the act of love, whose skills would press me to undreamt ecstasy. I'd expected to forget the world in her arms, in my lust.

But no. Only this fleshy, feathered *thing*.

Her gleaming eyes seemed to goggle. "What do you want?" she asked me.

I perused the terrifying, decadent creature and tried to regain my confidence, fighting back nausea and fear.

"I thought you'd be different," I said.

"I will take that other form should the moment merit," came the reply. "Now again, *what do you want?*"

"You," I said.

"Oh, you do?" she said.

I babbled, struggling to articulate the nature of my desire. "Yes. Nobody has ever... I mean, you, uh... Yes. Yes—"

She stared at me with her too-naked eyes. "You're not the first. There have been others. Many men and women like yourself, who've sampled and hungered for more."

"You know what I've dreamed. You—"

The creature raised a neotenous webbed hand. Her lips curled back in a predatory grin. "There are conditions."

"...Yes?"

"Oh, yes. You must travel to Raptor Mesa if you wish to experience my affection again. Forsake all other treasures, all other attachments, and offer yourself to me there. Will you promise?"

I looked at the wings and the hooked talons, my tongue deficient.

"*Why?*" I asked at last. "Why are you doing this to me?"

She stared at me, unblinking, unflinching.

"*Will you promise?*" she asked again.

I thought of her face and I thought of her hair and I thought of the way she'd smiled at me in my teens. And against all the psychological and anthropological logic in the world, I knew that I was in love with her. Well, maybe not in *love*, maybe not actually in *love*, not the way I loved Elizabeth. But she had looked into my eyes and smiled at me and wafted past in beguiling currents of vanilla, and in those first ten seconds with her I had experienced more excitement, more curiosity, more plain, straightforward *desire* than I had in the last year.

Supposing I get dressed and leave, I thought. *I'll spend the rest of my life wondering...*

"I promise," I said.

"There'll be no going back. You understand that?"

I wanted to kill her then. But not as much as I wanted her to love me.

"*I promise.*"

She needed no further vow. Her tongue darted out to spear the pigeon and she disappeared into the mirror. For a moment, I thought I glimpsed the woman, walking away into nothing...

An owl shrieked, somewhere.

Then all was still.

I stared at the mirror—a normal, safe mirror again—trying at first to find her again, and then to detect any signs of emotional breakdown in myself. But did it show on your face when you cracked, or was it all kept inside? Did it snap in the back of your brain where nobody could see?

I imagined Elizabeth sitting on the sofa sewing and glancing at the clock every few minutes, wondering where I was, calling my cell—I'd turned it off upon arriving at the house—maybe even calling the cops. I could see her opening the front door and smiling and kissing me and asking where I'd been, telling me how worried she and Baby had been…

And I remembered what it was like to worry about her, when she didn't answer.

I shrugged on my coat and went downstairs.

***

I found Elizabeth on her knees in the bathroom, sobbing over the toilet. I walked in and held her in my arms for five minutes before she could tell me what happened.

She'd swallowed rat poison.

I called the doctor, then left a message for Elizabeth's boss at the campus library, then returned to her side. Her depression had taken a turn for the worse in recent weeks. She'd stopped seeing her therapist, without telling me, because—as she told me between wracking sobs—the last few sessions had been less and less helpful.

And then I hadn't come home after work and she hadn't been able to reach me.

The two months that followed were painful. Elizabeth had vomited the poison up before it could do her permanent physical damage, but it was the first time she'd ever actually made an attempt like this. When I went back in to see her that day after the doctor gave me leave, we both collapsed in tears and held each other for hours.

Different meds and more frequent sessions with a new therapist helped a little, and group sessions brought her together with other survivors who had attempted suicide. Still, her recovery was slow. She was "granted" a non-negotiable psychological leave of absence from school and therefore work, but our home life suffered. We were still able to cover expenses—if only just—but neither of us felt comfortable with the other, especially in intimacy. It wasn't working. We talked and talked about it, but a settled taciturnity was absorbing us.

My nightmares intensified. Visions of Lilith in all her forms, now accompanied by memories of my terrible promise. A minute on the Internet informed me that Raptor Mesa was a tiny town in South Texas, a few miles east of the Mexican border.

I hadn't been to Texas since I was a little boy. That was on a family vacation, before the Wood King and the Divorce, when we passed through the Panhandle on the way to Arizona. The writing had been on the wall even then; Mom and Dad screaming at each other in a hotel, Dad slamming his open palm against the wall so hard that one of the room's generic landscapes had fallen to the floor and busted its frame.

Elizabeth began to speak of an unintelligible muttering in my sleep and a bizarre chanting that chilled her with a sense of unexplainable terror. Even Baby displayed a slight aversion toward me.

I suggested to Elizabeth that we get away from town for a while; maybe restful, rural surroundings would be the best thing for her full recovery. Besides, Dad—who, by then, had been living up north with his girlfriend for almost two years—had been offering to rent us the castle at a low rate since we'd first started looking for a place. Now, the situation being what it was, he offered to let us stay there rent-free.

When we drove out to look at it, Elizabeth was not enthusiastic. The place was somewhat weathered and weed-grown, fourteen miles outside town, and rather cheerless with the drawbridge up and the little moat long dry—in more than a year, Dad had only been down a handful of times to check on the place, and most of those visits had lasted less than a single day. I hadn't been there much myself after high school. Now it brought back a comforting flood of nostalgic memories from the better parts of my childhood.

"It's not quite what I had in mind," Elizabeth said as we stood in the hallway. It was twilight, an unseasonably chilly Monday in September. Not the ideal time to view a house that had been left empty so long.

"It needs a little work," I said. "That's all."

She shrugged.

"Don't worry," I said, going to where she was standing and wrapping my arms around her. "We can clean it up and make it like heaven."

"I don't know. Maybe."

"Trust me," I said.

"I do."

"All right then. What say we start moving in on Sunday?"

She nodded, but looked less than persuaded. I immediately began working out arrangements with my professors and my boss.

***

On Tuesday, I returned to Lilith's house with *The Outsider and Others* and a three-gallon can of gasoline. I splashed gas on the bare kitchen table, on the moldering living room chairs and cobwebbed mantelpiece, and drizzled it behind me as I ran back upstairs. A gray cat, ribcage-thin, bolted from a dark corner with half a garter snake in its mouth. I emptied the rest of the gas can on the mattress, gathered up the loose paper scraps, bunched them together in several places throughout the house—supplemented with torn out pages of Lovecraft—and emptied my matchbook lighting them. Nobody could be allowed to stay in that house, to find any clues about what had once lived there, what had transpired.

I didn't stay to watch, but the smoke rising in my rearview was satisfying enough.

Part Three: Some of Him Lived

9

For the rest of the week, I made the trip alone to clean up the castle with Dad. I didn't want Elizabeth to see it. She'd be surprised. When it was time to move in, I left a day early to see to last-minute details and picked her up the next day after Dad went back north. We planned to retrieve her car later that week.

The fire got a brief mention in the news, but more as a curiosity than a crime. The reporter almost seemed more surprised by the notion of a house there at all than its burning. If there was an investigation, I doubted its full-heartedness.

It was a crisp early-October day when I headed north on Interstate 74 with Elizabeth beside me in the Buick. In the back, Baby stood with her front paws braced on the seat and her face thrust into the wind from the open window.

"Do you want me to roll up the window?" I asked.

Elizabeth moved her head, letting the wind play with her loose brown hair. "No, it feels good. Clean."

We left the freeway for a two-lane blacktop road that snaked between vast, partially harvested cornfields. Trees soon replaced these and the outside air grew chilly.

As we drove on the forest pushed in closer on both sides of the road. The air was pungent with the scent of it.

Elizabeth reached out and touched my hand. "Pull over a minute, can you?"

Just before the road started over a bridge, I eased the Buick onto the shoulder and parked next to the metal guardrail. Below us lay a narrow river, wreathed with honey locusts.

Elizabeth lit a cigarette. She'd smoked a little in high school and had resumed the habit since the suicide attempt. I didn't like it, but I knew better than to fight her on it now.

She took a long drag, then mashed the cigarette into the ashtray. When she spoke again, the words came out in a rush. "Isaac, I *try*. I go through all the motions. But that's it, that's all I *can* do. There's no feeling and you know it. You can't help it. You've been sweet and patient with me, but I can't expect you to put up with this forever. I'm just not getting any better."

I said nothing for a moment. Then, "Did the therapist give you any advice?"

"Nothing I couldn't have gotten out of a magazine or off the Internet. Good, sound, logical advice, but I still don't feel anything."

"Give it a while," I said. "Two months isn't much time."

She nodded.

"Anyway," I went on, "that's what we're moving out here to the woods for, isn't it? Rest and rejuvenation?"

With what I hoped was an encouraging smile, I started the car, pulled back onto the road, and drove on. The clouds loomed up behind and cut off the sun. The air grew cold, and we rolled up the windows. As we drew nearer the castle, I switched on the headlights against the gathering gloom and drove slowly along past the trees, which already had a dead, uninhabited look.

Elizabeth shivered again.

I eased the Buick along another hundred yards, then braked to turn as the mouth of the castle's long driveway appeared from the shadows. The wide gravel path into the woods was still dotted with a few dead weeds.

The castle was dark and hidden from the road by the trees, which now towered up around us to pierce the slate-gray sky. We came at last to the clearing where the building itself stood and I parked behind Dad's ancient, dilapidated van which had remained undisturbed since he'd first moved away.

"Wait'll you see inside," I said, and thought I saw a hint of a smile on Elizabeth's face.

I got out of the car and walked back to open the trunk. I brought out her bags as she unlocked the kitchen door and turned on the porch light.

Baby put her nose out for a tentative sniff of the surroundings, then bounded out of the car and frolicked around my feet. I knelt and scratched her ear.

Inside I set the bags down on the sparkling kitchen floor and gestured Elizabeth into the living room. It and the open dining area were spotless and lit with colorful new lamps. The dark old furniture had been cleaned, polished, and recovered in bright hues, the carpet vacuumed and shampooed. Vases of fresh-cut flowers were everywhere.

I stood back and let Elizabeth survey the rooms. She walked through the dining area, running her fingers over the satiny finish of the heavy oak table.

"Well, what do you think?" I asked, unable to conceal my pride.

"Isaac, it's beautiful," she said, putting her arms around me. "I mean it."

"Thanks," I said. "How about some dinner? There're steaks in the fridge and martini makings in the pantry."

She stood on tiptoe and kissed me on the cheek. "Sounds tempting."

I got a blaze crackling over the artificial logs in the stone fireplace, then I went into the kitchen and took out the steaks. I brought back a bowl of ice, a green hydrant bottle of Tanqueray, and a bottle of vermouth, all of which I set before Elizabeth on the low coffee table in front of the fireplace. As I stirred the cocktails in a tall pitcher, Baby began to whine and scratch at the baseboard near the kitchen door.

"I think it's time she took a trip outside," I said. I crossed the room and held the door open. "Come on, Baby, out."

The little dog looked up at me, then at Elizabeth.

"Do you think she'll be all right?" Elizabeth said.

"Sure. There's no traffic out here and she won't go far enough to get lost."

Baby crouched lower to the floor, her eyes on me.

"Come on, you, *out*," I said again.

The dog obeyed at last, moving at a cautious creep. I closed the door after her, then sat down again and finished stirring the martinis. I brought out two iced glasses and filled them at the coffee table. We touched glasses, sipped at the cocktails, and smiled at each other.

"Did you get everything worked out at work?" Elizabeth asked.

"It's all taken care of. I've got next year's publication list to go over. When I go into town, I'll bring back whatever raw copy there is for editing. There's no reason those books can't be edited up here in the woods as well as on campus. I shouldn't have to make the trip into Baraigne more than once or twice a week, if that often."

Elizabeth leaned back on the sofa. "Are you sure you want to be cooped up here away from town and our friends?"

"We're not cooped up. We can go into town whenever we want. Think you'll miss battling through traffic twice a day? Listen," I squeezed her hand, "think of this as a vacation."

She leaned over and kissed me on the cheek again. "Didn't you say something about dinner?"

"Right," I said. "I'll get the steaks going, you make a salad."

"Do we have everything?"

"We should. I stocked up."

We ate together at the big oak dining table while shadows cast by the fire danced across the walls. After dinner, we relaxed on the sofa, drinking Dad's rich burgundy out of his big tulip glasses, feeling older than we were.

After I'd rinsed off the dinner dishes and stacked them in the sink, I joined her back in the living room.

We both started at the sound of something scraping at the kitchen door.

"Baby," I said, relaxing with a little laugh. "We forgot all about her."

I walked over and opened the door. The little dog dashed into the room and across the carpet to the couch. There she jumped up and pressed close to Elizabeth, peering back toward the door with wide brown eyes.

"She looks scared," Elizabeth said.

I stepped outside and looked both ways in the darkness. "Nothing out here."

I came back in and closed the door. Baby stayed close to Elizabeth on the sofa. We talked for a while about nothing important while the artificial logs in the fireplace burned.

I stretched my arms up over my head and yawned. "I don't know about you, but I'm ready for bed. We've got fresh, clean blankets upstairs, you know."

Elizabeth stiffened. "Maybe I'll have a cup of Sleepytime tea first." Her light tone of voice rang false.

She took as long as she could with the tea, then gave me a forced smile. "I'm tired too," she said. "Let's go to bed."

In the bedroom upstairs, I turned back the bright patchwork quilt and the snowy top sheet. Elizabeth hesitated, then undressed quickly. She slipped into bed beside me and pulled up the covers. Maybe it would be all right.

It wasn't. As soon as we were together in the big, comfortable bed and I put my hand on her, I felt a shiver spread throughout her body. Elizabeth squeezed her eyes shut and clasped her arms about her shoulders.

I pulled away.

"Oh," she said. "What's wrong with me?"

"Just that you keep thinking something is."

"I'm sorry."

"Cut it out. Everything'll be fine, long as we don't force it. Just get some sleep. Everything'll work out."

Hours later, as we lay not-quite-touching in the cold, predawn darkness, I heard the screech owls.

***

Morning came slowly to the castle. The blackness of the bedroom lightened almost imperceptibly until, at last, a finger of sunlight jabbed through a gap in the curtains. I lay awake for a long time waiting for Elizabeth to stir while the gray crept into the room. At last, her eyes opened. She looked over at me and smiled.

"Good morning," she said, rolling on her side to kiss me lightly on the mouth. "Sleep well?"

"Sure, I guess so." I reached over and patted her hip. "Let's have some breakfast."

Elizabeth swung out of bed. "You go ahead and shower, I'll set up in the kitchen."

Together we prepared and ate a breakfast of plump country sausages, eggs over easy, buttered rye toast, home fried potatoes, and coffee. The food along with the crisp morning air put me in a better mood.

Baby chowed on a helping of canned dog food with a fresh egg beaten into it. She ate as hungrily as we did, and afterwards dashed outside.

The house was always silent, except when we spoke, or when we played music. Pink Floyd, Rod Stewart, Kate Bush, Alice Cooper, Bruce Springsteen, some stuff from the '90s, some newer stuff, sometimes even Mozart or Beethoven. The walls were white and bare, the carpets gray. Even after cleaning it up, the castle seemed bleaker than I remembered. An anxious fortress of gray brick. Outside, the wind blew like a constant headache.

We went for walks in the woods, coat collars raised against the relentless chill. Baby circled around and around, yapping at us. We ate silent meals of meat and bread and cold white wine.

The chattering nightbirds outside disturbed me, a legion of screech owls crying an endless message.

Maybe I was going mad.

After midnight, their screams burst into a kind of cachinnation and not until dawn did they quiet down. Then they'd vanish, hurrying away until the next night.

On the third morning, I woke up and saw Elizabeth awake already, watching me. I reached out and stroked her hair.

She grinned at me, her old warm grin, and I felt a rush of affection for her. I leaned over and kissed her.

Saying nothing, I eased myself out from under the quilt and walked through to the bathroom. I switched on the light over the sink and inspected myself. I looked tired. But there was something else about my face which made me frown, a different cast about it. I stared at myself for a long time, but I couldn't decide what it was. I filled the sink with hot water and squirted a handful of shaving-foam into my hand.

Elizabeth and I both started as Baby dashed in through the open bedroom door and skidded to a stop, legs braced, ready to play.

"Looks like someone wants a walk," Elizabeth said, reaching down from the mattress to scratch the little dog behind the ear.

We got dressed and took her around the lane a few times. Sunlight filtering through the honey locust boughs gave the castle a hazy, unreal appearance. The trees sighed under a gentle breeze. Baby bounded ahead of us, always staying within a few yards. Watching her, Elizabeth touched my arm.

***

That night in bed, Elizabeth twisted and moaned under me. She dug her nails into my back. She caressed me with her hands and with her mouth. She heaved her body to meet mine and clamped her legs around my waist. She cried out for me to come inside her.

And I knew she felt nothing.

I tried to go along with her at first. I gripped her and tongued her ear and tried to say the right things so she wouldn't know I knew, wouldn't think her performance wasted. But I couldn't keep going, couldn't finish. After a while, I held her away from me.

"What's wrong?" she said.

"I'm tired," I said, hoping she'd believe me.

"No, you're not," she said. "What is it?" I could hear her frustration.

"It's okay," I said. "We don't have to keep going."

"What?"

"I know you're not into it."

"Yes, I—" she began, but cut herself off with a harsh sigh.

"It's okay," I said again, really meaning it.

"Jesus," she sat up. "I'm just trying to make you happy. Come on."

"I can't," I said. "I mean, I don't want to do it if you—"

"Let's just get it over with," she said. "Just let me get you off so I don't have to feel like a shitty girlfriend." She reached for me.

"No," I said, stopping her hand with mine. "It's really oka—"

"*Stop saying that,*" she said. "Just stop it."

"I'm sorry," I said. "I just—"

"I know," she said, rolling over. "Me too."

Soon she was asleep. I tried to sleep too, but as the minutes ticked into hours I gave it up and lay waiting, listening. I knew it would come, sure as death. And it did. The night cry of the owls.

After that, I slept fitfully, waking up time and again to listen to the night. At last, I woke with a start to find that it was light and Elizabeth was gone from the bed. I smelled coffee percolating in the kitchen and hurried to join her.

That day, and the next, and the next, Elizabeth and I didn't go into town. We stayed close to the castle, walking on the trails in the forest and delighting in the birds. Baby loved these outings. She would rush ahead barking at anything that moved, as though clearing the path for her people. Although Elizabeth and I kept up the pretense of enjoying each other, I suspected thoughts we couldn't share occupied us both.

In the evenings, we played cards, board games, and classic Nintendo gems. Having no cable and shoddy Wi-Fi, we rediscovered old favorites like *Eraser* and *RoboCop* in Dad's dusty VHS collection. Sometimes Elizabeth read from the stack of paperbacks she'd brought, while I worked at the kitchen bar going over the university's list of publications.

At night, we kissed goodnight and turned away from each other. While she slept, I would lie on my side, muscles taut, and stare into the dark.

Every night now, the screeching came. Elizabeth never seemed to hear it. I was afraid that if I talked about it, she would say it was all in my head. I knew better. It was more than just the owls. *She* was out there.

I began to walk in the forest by myself, telling Elizabeth I wanted to gather wood for the outdoor fire pit. We both knew there was all the wood we needed within fifty yards of the castle, but I don't think she minded the time away from me. I looked for the Wood King's hut, but never found it. One day I did find the blackened honey locust tree with the crude X still visible in the bark. Some animal had unearthed the chest and chewed through the Ziploc bag. The chest itself, despite some fungal growth on the wood and rust on the hinges, remained latched and intact. I took it into the garage and opened it, marveling over its forgotten contents. After finding the chest, I started carrying that old, never-used hunting knife in my jacket pocket, as much a talisman of my youth as an actual defensive weapon. I'd asked Dad to remove his guns before we'd moved in, thinking it would be the best thing for Elizabeth. Sometimes in the woods, or at night, I regretted that decision.

I made a habit of locking the bedroom door. I also began the precaution of making a brief search through the room, checking every shadow.

With these measures taken, I'd get into bed and fall asleep, with a nightlight glowing in the corner of the room. An old habit, resurrected from childhood. But dreams come through stone walls, darken lit rooms, and laugh at locks.

One night I dreamed I was in our bedroom, lying in bed, just as I was. I saw the room and its furniture as I had seen it last, except it was very dark, and something moved at the foot of the bed. It was a sooty-black animal that resembled a monstrous bird, about four or five feet tall. It continued back and forth with the restlessness of a caged beast. I could not cry out, though I was terrified. Its pace quickened and the room darkened even further. I could no longer see anything but its eyes. It sprang onto the bed. The two broad eyes approached my face and I felt a stinging pain as if two large needles darted deep into my chest. I woke with a scream and turned on the bedside lamp.

Once I was able to breathe and move, I hurried to check the door and found it locked as usual on the inside. I was afraid—horrified—to open it. I leapt into bed and covered my head up in the bedclothes, and lay there half-awake till sunup.

Every morning I experienced the same lassitude, and a torpor weighed on me all day. I felt changed. A strange melancholy was stealing over me. My own sort of depression settled and an idea that I was slowly sinking took gentle—and, somehow, not unwelcome—possession of me. Whatever it was, my soul acquiesced to it.

Certain vague and strange sensations also visited me in my sleep. The prevailing feeling was of a pleasant, peculiar cold thrill, as though swimming naked against the current of a river. The accompanying interminable dreams were so vague that I could never remember their scenery, cast, or even much of their action. They left me feeling awful and exhausted, as if I'd passed through an extended period of great mental exertion and danger.

After all these dreams, I recalled being in a dark place, conversing with people I couldn't see; and one clear voice, Lilith's, very deep and slow, speaking as if at a distance and always provoking the same fear. Sometimes I felt a huge hand drawn along my cheek and neck. Sometimes I felt warm lips kiss me, starting at my face and working down my throat, but then I'd wake with my heart beating practically out of my chest, sometimes gasping, sometimes sobbing.

I grew pale, my eyes dilated and darkened underneath. Elizabeth started asking if I was sick. I assured her I was fine. In a sense, this was true. I had no pain, no real physical complaints. Horrible as my sufferings were, I kept them, with a morbid reserve, as much to myself as I could. I never saw a doctor. Perhaps I should have. Perhaps things would've been different. Probably not.

The day of my third trip into Baraigne, fearing Elizabeth would read my eagerness, I made a show of reluctance to leave our wilderness paradise. In the Buick's rearview mirror, I watched the castle disappear down the narrow lane with an increasing sense of unease.

Returning home that evening, I found Elizabeth making us roast beef sandwiches in the kitchen. She greeted me with an enthusiastic hug. She'd cleaned the windows, even though they hadn't needed it, and reorganized all the books. She'd even lit candles to provide an intimate glow.

The sandwiches were perfect and talk came easily. It was almost the way it had been before.

After dinner, Elizabeth fed Baby and let her outside while I poured brandy. We moved into the living room and sat close together by the fireplace. Our legs touched, and for the first time in months, I felt a surge of real desire for her.

She must have felt it too.

"Isaac," she said, "let's go to bed."

"Sleepy already?"

She shook her head, holding the warm pressure of her thigh against me. "Nope."

I looked at her for a moment, then took her into my arms and kissed her. She returned the kiss with feeling. Her hands on my back and the taste of her mouth excited me.

We stood up and I led her into the bedroom.

When we were lying together, Elizabeth rolled onto her side to face me. My hand roved down across her rib cage and up over the swell of her hip. She reached down and found me erect and hard. The touch of her hand was good. My fingers trailed down across her stomach and into the dark fluff of pubic hair.

Oh, God, I thought, *let it be good this time. Let it be right, the way it was.*

I was kissing her breast, teasing the nipple with my tongue. My hand was up between her legs, stroking, massaging. She was ready for me and I for her.

Then I heard the owls.

Not far off in the woods this time, but close outside. Close, and cold as death.

"Elizabeth!" I said, sitting up in bed.

"I hear it," she said. She pulled herself up beside me, but her voice did not reflect the urgency I felt.

Elizabeth's hand moved between my legs. Her head dipped to my chest.

"What is it?" I said. I was whispering without knowing why.

"I don't know. An owl." Her tone took on an edge of impatience.

"Not just an owl," I said.

"Who cares? Come on, babe, lie down."

I fell back on the sheet, tried hard to recover the mood, but the terrible screeching still sounded in my brain.

Elizabeth's head moved lower on my body. Her tongue traced a moist line to my navel...

And it was not Elizabeth kissing me there, it was that terrible *other* thing. The forked tongue in my flesh.

With a startled cry, I drew away from her.

She pulled herself up. "What?"

I reached out to her, trying to make my touch affectionate. "I'm sorry, Liz. I—I don't think I can."

"But just a minute ago—"

"I know," I said. "I know, Liz, but now I can't."

"*Fuck*," she said through clenched teeth and turned away from me, her naked back a low wall in the middle of the bed.

"Please, babe," I said, "I'm sorry."

She gave me an unconvincing pat on the shoulder. "Sure, Isaac, it's all right. It's just—I was working myself up for this all night. But you've been patient with me, so I should be with you."

It wasn't all right. We both knew it. My throat filled up with words I wanted to say to her but could not: *I'm sorry, I was all ready, in the mood, and then that screech. And then the only picture in my mind was that filthy creature with her tongue in me, her tongue biting me and...*

But I couldn't say that. I'd never spoken of that to anyone.

I forced my mind back from the brink of panic and, at last, fell into a shallow sleep.

***

I dreamed Lilith was caressing me and murmuring to me. I dreamed I was trying to run across a beach, across wide gray sands, but the sands turned to glue and clung around my ankles. I heard music, voices.

There was no escape.

I was lost. Living with a woman I feared I loved less and less, through little or no fault of her own.

And Lilith. Lilith was mystery, Lilith was darkness, Lilith was all I'd dreamed of. And if I would only go to her, she would free me. I would serve her, and in exchange, she would service me, love me, end this torment…

I opened my eyes. The house was silent.

I pulled on a pair of jeans and a heavy sweater and took Baby out for a breath of fresh air. The night was cold with a high overcast.

We walked around the corner to the front of the castle, Baby leaping ahead as always.

Away from the kitchen light, the dark was almost perfect and I was glad of it. My eyes rested against the night, their surfaces chilled.

Then, from the trees, I heard a sound.

It was no louder than the distant report of a bird flapping its wings from a high branch. After a few seconds, it stopped. I held my breath. It came again.

The noise awoke desperation in me.

I swallowed and spoke to the darkness.

"I hear you," I said, not sure why the words came, or to whom they were addressed.

The flapping ceased for a moment and then began again. I stepped away from the door and moved toward the noise. It continued as if summoning me.

It was easy to miscalculate in the dark, and I reached the wall of trees before I'd expected to. Raising my hands, I ran my palms over the peeling, uneven bark. The bird stopped flapping.

For a moment, I swam, disoriented, in darkness and silence. Something moved in front of me. A trick of the eye?

Only then did I realize that I'd been holding my breath and was becoming light-headed. I tried to empty my lungs of the stale air and take a gulp of fresh, but my body would not obey this simple instruction.

Somewhere in my innards, a tic of panic began.

Again, I tried to take a breath, but it was as if my body had died and I was staring out of it, unable now to breathe or blink or swallow.

The moonlight pierced the clouds and I saw something flicker across my field of vision, ragged enough to be a shadow but too substantial. Then the moon was blocked again.

The wild, fierce cries of Baby off in the dark roused me. Her high, terrible snarling mounted in volume and stopped almost at once. After a horrible pause, a different scream rang out—the scream that had haunted my dreams.

I rushed across the lane and through the trees but saw nothing in the black absence of moonlight. The barking and the screaming, now fast fading into a mixed low growling and moaning, proceeded from the darkness. These sounds, except for a droning whine from the dog, soon subsided. I now perceived with a sudden start that a loud chorus of screech owls among the shrubbery had commenced a rhythmic piping.

The trees were full of a terrible stench and I rushed to the place from which I thought the low whining came, calling Baby's name.

The owls shrieked in a final crescendo.

The clouds parted a second time, and against the moon, vast clouds of feathery watchers rose and raced from sight.

Baby was nowhere to be seen.

I called her name again and again. The forest was silent, the only sound the dripping of moisture from the tree branches. I walked all around the yard, whistling and calling for the little dog. Several times I edged into the woods, crying louder, and came back with my jeans wet from the damp brush.

I returned to the bedroom and shook Elizabeth awake.

"Baby's not here," I said. "I took her out and now I can't find her. She doesn't answer. I looked all over." I sensed the rising pitch of my voice, but I did not try to control it. Concern for the dog was an acceptable outlet for the other tangled emotions I wasn't ready to examine.

"Do you think something happened to her?"

"She's probably off exploring somewhere," I said without conviction. "What could happen? We've been here over two weeks. Baby knows her way around by now. She'll come home when she gets hungry, right?"

Elizabeth insisted on looking again and we went out together with flashlights for another hour. Nothing answered.

***

In the morning, I was the first one up. I ran a comb through my hair and went into the kitchen. I made breakfast for Elizabeth—a ham-and-cheese omelet with hot English muffins and rich black coffee. But first I put an open can of Alpo on the kitchen porch in case Baby was still near enough to smell it. I left the door open a crack, despite the cold.

While I was cooking the omelet, Elizabeth came down. From time to time, each of us would look over toward the door.

Afterward, I went to work editing manuscripts. Elizabeth sat in a chair by the window, reading. I tried to focus, but the printed words would not register in my mind and I had trouble sitting still.

"Isaac," she said just before noon. "I think we should go out and look for her again. Maybe she's hurt and can't get back to us."

I looked over at her, hoping she would see my thankfulness for the interruption as genuine concern.

"All right," I said.

The sun was out now, high and pale, but warm enough to dry off the forest. Elizabeth and I walked the trails that interlaced the surrounding woods. Some were so dim and overgrown that they were hardly there. Others showed signs of more recent use.

I went in one direction, Elizabeth in another. I concentrated on looking down as I walked, scanning the ground along both sides of each trail. I saw nothing.

Elizabeth must've done the same. When I came upon her suddenly walking from the opposite direction, she started and gave a little squeal of surprise.

I reached out and grasped her arm gently. "No luck?"

She shook her head and turned away.

I put my arms around her and held her.

We took a short drive up and down the road, going a couple of miles each way. We didn't talk. There was no sign of Baby in the roadway or in the brush alongside.

I kept my eyes straight ahead as I turned back toward the castle, but I could see Elizabeth glancing over at me.

"What if a coyote got her?" she asked, on the verge of tears again.

"We can't think about that," I said.

***

It turned even colder the following week. An Arctic chill brought on a light but steady snow that covered the ground in a handful of days. We put up posters in town, scoured the woods and the roads every day.

I worried Baby had already frozen to death, but I didn't dare voice my thoughts to Elizabeth. What would she do, when she lost hope? The thought terrified me, but I knew the day would come eventually. I didn't want to know.

At night, we didn't even try to make love. I stayed up long after Elizabeth, working, I told her. When I finally went into the bedroom, I was careful not to wake her and immediately went to sleep. She started wearing pajamas to bed, breaking a years-long habit of sleeping in just a t-shirt. I pretended not to notice.

The last time we searched for Baby in the woods, the snow was several inches deep. As the afternoon crept into early evening, we split up to cover more ground before nightfall could force us back inside.

I walked in the opposite direction Elizabeth had gone, calling Baby's name until my voice became hoarse. Elizabeth's similar cries echoed through the cold, among the stripped, frosted trees. I crossed the little black stream, now frozen solid, and walked until I could barely hear Elizabeth's echoes over the crunch of snow underfoot.

My eyes ranged over the ground. Nothing stirred in the bright orange light of early sunset. Many tracks disturbed the uneven white blanket: deer, rabbits, birds ranging in size from sparrow to crow. And then—

Dog tracks. Just about the right size for Baby. Or a young coyote.

I reached into my pocket for the knife and followed the tracks.

Maybe there is hope. Maybe it is Baby, maybe she is alive. Maybe it is her...

All at once I was sure it *must* be her. I'd find her soon, emaciated but alive, sniffing around in the snow for an unlucky mouse or a frozen opossum. I imagined Elizabeth's joy as I met her back at the castle, Baby trembling and hungry in my arms.

We'd warm her up, feed her, take her to the vet for a checkup, and everything would be okay.

The tracks led me into a small, familiar clearing.

The ruined, roofless hut waited near its center.

I stopped dead, stifling a scream that was as much surprise as it was genuine terror. The half-shaved sticks that had made up one wall were almost entirely gone, some of the plywood had been gnawed away along the edges, and a thin layer of snow dusted the whole thing. But it was unmistakable.

And it was occupied.

Not by the Wood King, but a forest beggar: a lean coyote. It faced away from me, its hindquarters protruding from behind one wall, its scrawny tail wagging. Its head remained hidden behind the frozen plywood, but I could tell it was eating something. What else could've so preoccupied it that it ignored my presence? I hadn't been stealthy in my approach, and even if by some miracle it hadn't heard me, it must smell me.

Oh God, what if it's eating her?

"Hey!" I drew the knife from my pocket.

The coyote flinched, and for a heartbeat appeared frozen in place. I wondered if it would fight or flee. Would I chase it, kill it, if it had killed Baby? Like some small-scale Midwestern version of Ahab and the whale?

It backed out of the hut, looked at me. I saw what it held in its jaws.

A squirrel. Headless and partially disemboweled, but also unmistakable.

The coyote ran with its meal, dashing between trees in an almost playful way. I watched it go until it blended with the forest.

When it was gone, I stood staring at the hut.

I had walked every acre of these woods more than once since we'd come here. I had followed the creek to either end of the property. There had been no trace of the hut then, not even a blank spot where it had once stood. The entire clearing might as well have been removed and replaced with a less remarkable patch of forest. Now it was all back, as though it had never vanished.

Why?

I took a tentative step toward it. Then another, and another, until I was standing at the threshold. I peered at the snow-covered floor. Beneath the snow, dozens of little clustered masses were lumped together in short piles. They looked almost like little pine cones, but I knew at once they were owl pellets. There was no smell in the freezing air, but I imagined they stank of vanilla.

Plywood cracked under my gloved hand and I realized I was leaning against the wall of the hut. I recoiled as though I'd touched a hot stovetop, almost falling over backwards in my revulsion.

The sun was now well below the tree line, and its orange rays filtering through the narrow trunks made me even more uneasy. Soon it would be too dark to see without a flashlight. I didn't want to be anywhere near here by then. I started back to the castle at a fast walk, forcing myself not to break into a dead run. Running would be a kind of admission, a kind of *sub*mission, to the hut and whatever still lurked there out of sight.

I didn't tell Elizabeth about the tracks or the hut or any of it. Knowing a hungry coyote was wandering the property might strangle whatever hope remained in her.

That night I had another dream of something black coming around the bed and I awoke thinking I saw Baby lying in the corner. It was only a shadow, cast through the window from the moonlight. When I looked to the window it was empty, but I heard a sort of muffled swishing or flapping sound from somewhere outside.

It was an effort not to scream, to voice my terror and frustration and anger together in a single sustained howl. Instead, I sat up awhile and cried in silence. I couldn't take it anymore.

The next morning, Elizabeth acted cheerful, obviously hiding a bad mood. I knew well enough to play along with her about it.

I wanted to run again. My heart pounded so furiously I was sure she must hear it. But no. She asked me if I wanted another cup of coffee. I said I did. Clearly pleased I hadn't asked her if she was okay, she brought me a refill and returned to her seat.

I hadn't known that would be the day. But, during this second cup, I said it.

"Uh, look, honey, something's come up with the manuscripts I brought home."

"Oh?"

Too late to turn back now.

"Yeah, looks like I'm going to have to run into town, meet up with the writer."

"Today?"

"Well, yeah, the sooner the better. You'll be all right?"

"Of course."

"Anything I can do for you before I go?"

"I'm not an invalid, Isaac."

"I hate to go."

I dabbed at my mouth and stood up, anxious to be on my way but trying not to show it. I gathered up the manuscripts and took them out to the car, grabbing my jacket on the way, with its comforting knife-weight in the pocket. Elizabeth walked out with me. She kissed me goodbye, then turned and walked back to the house as I drove away. I watched her in the rearview until she was out of sight.

At the end of the lane, I slipped a letter into the mailbox. I'd written it days before, in preparation for my leaving, though I hadn't been sure I'd ever use it:

> I'm too ashamed to tell you in person, and I think I'll break down if I hear your voice, so I'm writing instead. I tried to be strong for you, but I failed. I've become a cold, empty, miserable husk of my old self, and I've got to face the monster responsible. I ache, seeing you hurting as you are, and the last thing I want is to make things worse, but there is hope. I'm sorry for being so blind to your pain for so long, for being so arrogant and stubborn. I can't write or think collectedly now. I'm distracted. I mean to go as far as Texas, hopefully no farther. I will see you again soon—that is, if you'll let me. I'll tell you everything then. Goodbye. Pray for me, love.

On my way to I-30 West, I took a short detour. Lilith's house had indeed burned to the ground and no trace of life lingered amongst the blackened ruins. Only a stench and a tarry stickiness that filled me with an odd sense of pride. Even the horse paddock—the only thing I hadn't burned—had finally collapsed. I left my phone amongst its rotting timbers.

Part Four: It's Coming to Know

10

In an otherwise-empty tavern called Hackler's, an old man stared at me.

I'd driven through the night, speeding the whole way. In thirty minutes, I'd covered the forty-mile stretch from I-35 to the small, abandoned-looking strip club that marked the edge of Raptor Mesa, and the aggregation of trailers and small houses that made up the better part of the town. I'd checked in to the local apology for a motel—the kind that doesn't even have a name—on Sunshine Lane and taken a deep, dreamless nap before setting out for some lunch.

The white-haired, ruddy-faced man sat at the bar with a glass of beer in front of him. He looked at me, his face expressionless, and his piercing black eyes sent a chill up my spine. In them I read a cold, malevolent fury.

The man's fixed gaze unsettled me, but there was something familiar about it. So familiar, in fact, as to be almost comforting in this strange place. In any case, I was hungry and this appeared to be the only place open.

I sat down at a table for one near the window, about as far as I could get from the bar. I took a look at the menu: a small, one-sided card with three items on it, laminated in fingerprint-smudged plastic that curled and peeled at the corners.

"What'll ya have?" the bartender called.

The old man watched me.

Just let me eat my lunch in peace.

I ignored the unrelenting stare, ordered a breaded pork tenderloin and a beer. I dug into the sandwich and for a moment forgot everything but the bliss of warm food in my mouth, dry and bland though it was.

"So, you've come after all."

I almost choked. I looked up to see the old man standing over me. Tall and slender and very near in his rumpled blue business suit and scuffed shoes, leaning on a slim black cane. He wore a small, humorless smile and his eyes twinkled as he dabbed his forehead and beard with a handkerchief.

"Huh?" I said, gulping my beer to keep from coughing.

"Never saw Her go to anyone like that before," he said, putting the handkerchief somewhere in his jacket, which looked maybe a size too small for him. He spoke with a faint Southern accent. "Not like that. And then you still didn't come and I thought, *maybe*..." His voice trailed off and he shrugged. "But here you are."

I noticed a knife-scar across his left cheek, extending upward over the temple and into his hair; a bald streak showing the trail of the steel in his scalp.

"W-who are you?"

"You don't remember me?" he said. "I shouldn't be surprised. I'm not, really. Guess I just...hoped—" He cut himself off with a soft chuckle.

I stared at him and remembered. His hair was different—whiter, thinner—and the scar was new, as were the bristling mustache and patchy beard. But those fierce, unwinking eyes and predatory nose were the same.

"The farmhouse," I said. "You were with her."

The man nodded. I'd never seen anyone look so grim before.

"You knew this was going to happen all along," I said. "Right from the very beginning. You *knew.*"

He nodded again. I should've been violent with rage. I should've seized him by the throat and beaten his head against the wall. But for some inexplicable reason I was terrified of touching him.

"I'm sorry for you," the man said. "Please believe me. But I'm just as sorry for myself. I used to be like you. Name's Cavallari. I used to go to school, play guitar. But then I was wounded, here—" he touched his chest "—and was never the same since. It gets harder to remember every year." He paused. "Like a diver, trying to see the sky through water. I think—I think my parents were from—was it Chicago? I—"

"Why didn't you warn me?" I said. "Why didn't you stop me from going upstairs with her?"

Cavallari seated himself on the extreme edge of the opposite chair and held his cane between his knees. I noticed the little finger on his left hand had been amputated close to the knuckle. Three plain gold rings, like wedding bands, decorated each large hand.

"For love," he said. "A cruel love, a strange love that will take my life. Or yours. Love will have its sacrifices. No sacrifice without blood."

"Yes," I said, and touched the knife in my pocket. "But why not her life? Her blood?"

He chuckled again, shaking his head.

"It's been happening for years," he said. "Decades. Centuries, probably."

Remembering the brooding presences around the castle and the dim, hideous aura that had stretched over the old Victorian house, I felt a wave of fright as cold as a graveyard draft. The man before me seemed like the spawn of another planet or dimension, linked to a bent, black gulf I had only glimpsed thus far.

"You're talking about Lilith?"

Cavallari nodded. "Lilith, Abyzou, Gyllou, Ishtar, all of Them. And Their Father."

"*Them?*" I gulped. Of course, I'd come across those names in my researches of years past, but I'd assumed them all to be manifestations or interpretations of the same solitary creature. The notion of more than one like her filled me with fresh dread. "Their…father?"

"You've heard of Hakim the Masked?"

I shook my head.

"Dyer of Merv," Cavallari said. "Al-Moqanna. That was He, veiled as a man."

"He?"

"The one from whom Lilith and the Others sprung. The Pallid One."

The Wood King.

I lowered my head, shivering. I'd wondered if there was a connection, but—had I been marked so young?

Cavallari brought me back to the present. "I could kill you," he said.

I reached into my pocket for the comfort of the knife, trying not to shiver again.

Cavallari didn't seem to notice. He looked thoughtful. "I could," he said with a vigorous double nod. "But what would that achieve? I mean, at least *you* would be out of my way—but there are already others." He paused, his eyes resting on me for only a moment before darting away like startled fish. "Well, now it's going to happen to you."

I felt a prickle of grave apprehension. "What is?"

Cavallari raised his head and began speaking in that strange, resonant fashion.

"She's been in love with no one and never shall," he whispered, "but you will always think yourself the exception to that rule, despite everything." He smiled again—a short, nervous smile that showed teeth too even to be real. "It's not murder to Her."

"I'll kill her," I said, a hand still in my pocket.

"I don't think so," Cavallari said. "Maybe you'll think about it, the way I thought about it long ago." He seemed about to stand, but then settled back in the seat and laid a hand on the table. "One man to the next. The man who was Her favorite before me—a man I *did* kill—he told me everything about it, just as I'm telling you."

"Yes?" I said, willing myself to relax a little.

He gave one end of his mustache a savage twist and launched right into it.

"I'd never noticed Her in my English class until that day. The Doors had just been on Sullivan the night before, and it was foggy out. She asked a question about *Beowulf*, sounding so shy, and when I glanced over my shoulder, I saw the prettiness of Her young face, that red hair. She was wearing a loose yellow sweater, practically swimming in it. As I turned back to my book, my heart started beating and my skin started crawling at the same time, but in an exciting way. I thought about Her all through the rest of class. She looked so petite, so innocent.

"Then the bell rang and, as we all left the classroom, She bumped into me and dropped her books. I picked them up and was about to ask Her out on a date when She said, 'Come to my place some evening. I'm free tonight.' She gave me the address on a scrap of paper and was gone before I could reply.

"It was an old, unremarkable Victorian house on the outskirts of Point Pleasant, stripped of its former cheap grandeur. It'd stood empty for a decade or more before She'd claimed it, and was forgettable in every way except it was *Hers*. There was rot in the cellar, and in the upper story the din of those owls never ceased. Almost rattled the windows, certainly rattled the mind. It was a haunted house—though no house is unhaunted once *She* takes it. There were a few roommates then, though not as many as at Baraigne when you arrived. All rather bohemian. I even saw one of the professors there, dying by inches.

"She gave me some of that red wine of Hers and we worked off our clothes and came together on Her ancient bed. Afterwards, as I sat up against a pillow, dripping sweat and watching the reddening sky through Her window, She shed Her disguise.

"Ah, the horrors we committed in that house. The place was shunned by most vermin. No mice crawled in its kitchen, only the owls nested in its attic. The violence we did there opened the place up like a gutted fish. Opened it to Her world, where the dead mingle. Two months later, I was in deep as the rest, but we were already getting too much notice. Some gravediggers and teenagers had glimpsed Her the year before, as only we had been permitted to see Her, and a couple a' dogs'd gone missing."

I'm not sure if he caught my look at that, but he did pause before continuing. "People all over the state were getting nosy. It was fortunate for us that the Silver Bridge collapsed when it did. We were able to move on without drawing attention." He paused again, looking thoughtful. "Her oldest living follower then was an ex-Nazi She'd met in Veracruz in the fifties. Weltz, his name was. She'd brought him into America with Her. I killed him in the summer of—oh, I don't even remember when now. Hell, you mightn't've been born.

"It's gone on year after year. She's been through hundreds since I've known Her. Each one's different, but they're all the same. Some women, more men. Easier to take, I guess. Many tried to escape. Business executives, cops, soldiers, scientists—even priests. Some resisted Her for months or years, others succumbed after fewer than two days. Only a small few haven't come back, and I suspect they might yet. She's a collector of weak souls, gathering us up, little victims of our own making."

I only nodded.

He pounded the table. "She feels nothing for you or me, while what we feel for Her erodes our very dignity. It's a pathetic, miserable, begging adoration that longs for reciprocation. We amuse Her, but we're not special to Her."

I only nodded and again he gave me that little smile. A wicked smile.

Is Lilith watching this?

My eyes strayed to the window, ranged along the plain-white front of the King's Way Temple across the street.

Yes, she's here. She sees. She knows.

I felt myself trembling.

I hesitated briefly and then stood. He stood too and stared at me with hostility in his eyes that I'd never seen from anybody before. He looked quite capable of killing me.

He made an indecisive move in my direction. I skirted his touch.

"Go away," he said, and I heard his voice catch. "All I'm asking you to do is go away. It'll be better for both of us."

Almost before he'd finished speaking, he was moving out the door at a brisk walk, the cane all but forgotten. I stayed put, watched him through the window as he got into a rusty white Dodge Challenger across the street and tore off, out of sight. I didn't catch the license plate, but I memorized the car.

Maybe I should've followed him then, gotten it over with. But I didn't. I got another beer, settled up, and went back to the motel. I took a shower, even though I'd brought no clean clothes to change into. I put the dirty ones back on, socks and underwear inside-out.

What will Elizabeth do without me? The thought stopped me cold like a bullet in the brain. I stared at myself, bleary and half-dressed in the mirror, and began to weep with rage. *You've started to accept it already. You're not going back. You've already forgotten that you love her. You wanted to propose to her...*

Exhausted, I sat down on the floor and sobbed until I was too tired to cry.

My sleep was good, long and dreamless. When I woke it was well past midnight, but I felt refreshed. I picked up a paperback novel I'd brought: an old Lancer Books edition of *Ayesha*. It seemed appropriate.

After a couple of hours, I tossed the book aside and got up, finished getting dressed. I opened the door, switched off the light, and hung my jacket over my shoulders. In its pocket, the knife. The sun was just beginning to rise.

I took my car back down Temple Street in the direction I thought Cavallari had taken, looking for that white Challenger, but it didn't seem to be anywhere.

I passed a mornings-only cafe and the town's only gas station on Hawk Street, both vacant of customers. A boarded-up theater on Beacon Street advertised "H D I H RRO" on an otherwise empty marquee. A faded poster in a glassless frame identified the movie as *The Dunwich Horror*.

Nothing in Raptor Mesa seemed to do much business.

I circumnavigated the entire town, scanning driveways—a process which, even at my slow pace, took all of twenty minutes—and was almost back where I'd started when I saw a small, out-of-place-looking copse of evergreens down South Jab Street and decided to investigate. The town ended more-or-less at the intersection of South Jab and Catfish Drive, and the road ended unceremoniously in the rocky dust and brown grass just beyond those trees. Among them, I saw the gap-toothed picket fence and broken shutters of a tumbledown house, not unlike the one I'd burned. Parked in the shade on either side were an old gray Volvo, two dirty pickup trucks, and—

The Challenger.

The wind moaned among the black boughs of the pine trees as I ran toward the house. Though the sun had risen, I felt a chill about me as I climbed the sagging steps of the old building's ruined veranda and paused, breathless, before the unpainted front door.

I leaned forward and tried the doorknob with a light, tentative touch. The door gave under my hand, swinging inward on protesting hinges, and I tiptoed into a dark, dust-carpeted hall. Once inside it took a few moments to adjust to the gloom. A shaft of new sunlight, slanting downward from a chink in one of the window shutters, showed innumerable dust motes flying lazily in the air, and laid a bright oval of light against the warped floorboards.

Where the sunbeam splashed on the uneven floor, I saw the mark of a booted foot—a trail of them leading toward the rear of the house.

I reached into my jacket pocket and followed the trail through the gloomy hall, stepping carefully to avoid creaking boards as much as possible. The marks stopped in the center of what was once the kitchen. At the old table sat a muscular young Mexican man not far from my own age and a thin woman with blond hair that ended just above her shoulders. I remembered her from the Illinois house and smiled in spite of myself. The two of them had been playing cards with a worn deck in the light from the kitchen window, but now they sat still, staring at me. I froze and looked back at them, clutching the knife in my pocket, but they said nothing and made no move to get up. I recognized something in their eyes. They seemed to recognize something in mine.

Deciding they wouldn't attack me, I looked around the room. A ringbolt in the floor revealed that I stood above some kind of trapdoor. I glanced back at the card players. They watched me with an air of mild boredom. I bent, seized the rusty ringbolt, and heaved the trapdoor up. I had to take my hand from my pocket as I slid down and wondered if the two would rush me then. They didn't.

I eased the trapdoor closed above me and stared into the room ahead.

The cavern had been a cellar for the storage of food; brick-walled and earth-floored, without a window or ventilation, and lit by a single bare bulb. A dank, musty odor assaulted my nostrils as I leaned forward, but the sight before me blotted out further impressions.

Lilith's pale, bare body lay in sharp reverse silhouette against the darkness of the cavern floor, her ankles crossed and firmly lashed to a stake in the earth, the arms extended straight outward, wrists pinioned to other stakes. Her luxuriant red hair was knotted together at the ends and staked to the ground, drawing her head far back and exposing her rounded throat to its fullest extent.

Crouched over her was the babe-naked relic of a man, that old, wrinkled witch-husband, Cavallari, with matted white hair and beard. In one hand, he held a gleaming breast, while with the other he caressed Lilith's smooth throat with gloating strokes of his skeleton fingers. His body was pale and waxy, like a fungus. The skin on his upper chest and belly sagged, marked with old bite scars like chickenpox. He kissed her face, her arms...

Lilith looked up. Her bright eyes met mine, smiling.

The old man snatched his walking stick from the earth beside Lilith's pinioned wrist, but my hand was already in my jacket pocket. As he stood and stepped toward me, I turned on him, knife out. He paused, crouching like some subhuman creature, and I rushed him.

Cavallari gave ground with a quick, catlike leap that belied his frail appearance, grasping his cane in both hands near the top. In an instant, he ripped the lower part of the stick away to display a fine, three-edged blade set in the cane's handle. He swung his point toward me, baring his polished plastic teeth like a beast. His eyes gleamed like a dog's in the dim light.

I heard soft sighs of anticipation from Lilith. Somewhere, wings flapped.

Cavallari launched himself at me, stiffening his sword arm. I sank back on one foot, then lunged. His pace was too quick to avoid the blade and it sliced into his belly with ease. I opened one cut, then another.

As the blood started, the light flickered once. I saw Lilith trembling.

My breath froze in my throat.

Cavallari half turned, as though on an invisible pivot, let out a wheezing curse, and—instead of moving away—took a step toward me and knocked the knife from my hand with a slash of his own wire-fine blade. It spun across the floor toward the wall. He was upon me before it stopped.

He put his hand on my head and took a fistful of hair. It seemed his intention was no longer violence, but escape, for he let go as soon as he'd pulled me out of his way. I fell against the wall, looking up to see him moving toward the trapdoor, one hand clamped to his cuts.

I moved across to where the knife lay and back up toward him in the space of a second, bringing the knife down in the middle of his wrinkled back. He made a sort of gasping grunt. I was already drawing the knife out, plunging into him a second time, a third and a fourth. I lost count of the wounds I made, my attack lent venom by his refusal to die, his failure to stop me. I wondered, as I drove the blade into the reptile standing before me, why this was so very *easy*.

He stumbled around the room, crying and gurgling, blood running over his buttocks and legs and out of his mouth. After an age, he sank to his knees, keeled over, and hit the floor.

Almost as an afterthought, I registered that he'd stopped breathing. I crossed the blood-spattered floor to where he lay, wiped the blade on my pants, and stood over Lilith. She looked up at me, her expression one of mingled desire and triumph.

I crouched over her, knife in hand.

"Do you love me?" I heard her say. My eyes were on her pinioned arms, her exposed breast. I gripped the knife tight, smelling the familiar vanilla scent, and felt my own dreadful mix of triumph and repulsive longing.

Just one quick motion.

I moved the blade down.

With meticulous care, I cut her bonds.

I looked away as her tongue pierced Cavallari's throat, but I heard her orgasmic grunt, and I was almost tempted to run myself. The blood was already drying on my hands, its stickiness revolting.

The room became a furnace as she pumped the dead man's energies from his body. I watched, entranced, the corpse convulsing in the draining of every nutritious element. Gases shifted and moaned in its cavities and orifices, the already-shriveled skin desiccated even further in front of my eyes, and I imagined the innards being liquified and sucked out like a spider's dinner. The bulb flickered again. I looked away from her, toward the wall, and realized I would never see Elizabeth or Baby or the castle again.

As the room cooled again, I peered down at Cavallari's shrinking arm. The deterioration had slowed almost to a stop. She was still finding nutrients to squeeze from the body, sucking it clean of marrow and vital fluids.

The husk collapsed.

The sound of it undammed my panic. I began to shake and cry, the tears pouring like Cavallari's blood. I was sure I'd be sick. I was sure it would last forever.

I almost wish it had.

Now there's no sound from the gloom. Distant wings no longer flap. She's left little more than a small mass of whitish human dust on the floor, and sticky-looking fragments of dried flesh. Only the plastic teeth remain whole and unmarred. As she stands again, something shifts in the ever-closer shadows of the room. She is beautiful.

"Isaac," she says with a smile. "Much better."

"Yes," comes a broken voice from somewhere inside me. "It's me."

It's a tired voice—the voice of somebody used up—Cavallari's voice.

"It's all right," she whispers, soothing. "Oh, darling…"

Darling! I could laugh, but for my terror. I'm here if she wants me—her darling, her *sweetheart.*

"I don't want…" My words are halting, wretched. "I have to have you."

"I'm glad you came," she says.

I will never see Elizabeth or Baby or the castle—

"You're beautiful." I spit the words out as though they've vexed me for hours. "The most beautiful woman who ever lived."

—or Mom or Dad or the Big Beverly or Baraigne County…

"Take off your jacket. You're warm."

"I am," I say, but do nothing. She moves across to me and I tremble like a lamb. I shrug off my jacket at her light touch.

"Would you like to go upstairs?" she says. The words make my eyes burn.

"Yes," my voice says. "Yes. I'd like that."

As she comes closer, I hear a sound not unlike laughter from the darkness inside me, nor unlike sobs.

Epilogue

Elizabeth handled the following months of shadow and solitude as she had most of her post-pubescent life: with the outward appearance of composure. Those first few days and nights, talking to the police and Isaac's parents and her own family and friends, her anxiety and dread and unstrung nerves had briefly gotten the better of her. But once she'd packed her bags and gotten out of that castle, out of those woods, the pain began to lessen.

She had taken up residence in a cheap apartment in town—even smaller than the one she'd shared with Isaac before the castle—and secured a front-end job at the grocery store next door. With some assistance from her parents, she was able to continue with therapy and medication. She devoted herself to moving forward and, at least, to the appearance of health.

It had been more than six months since Isaac's departure. Since the shock of finding that note in the mailbox. Since the brief investigation had closed with the conclusion that Isaac had simply walked out on her, and didn't *want* to be found. And still there were no real answers. Only haunting speculation and frequent tearful awakenings from sleep. Why had he left? Fear? An attempt to escape something he perceived as horrible? Isaac had never struck Elizabeth as the type to do such a thing.

But he did, didn't he? You *drove him off. You and your problems. Your emptiness. It was all too much for him to bear, as it would be for any reasonable person. You weren't there for him the way he was for you, you didn't fuck him enough, you were too cold, too mean, too negative—*

No. Self-blame was pointless. He was gone and that was that. Hating herself wouldn't bring him back.

It's not your fault. That's what everyone kept telling her: her parents, her friends, her therapist. They were all there for her, or so they said. But her parents and friends treated her with kid gloves, as though afraid she might self-immolate at the slightest provocation. She'd grown to resent their overly concerned manners and tones. They made her feel burdensome rather than comforted, and only spiked her anxiety. She'd also noticed that her circle of friends, never large to begin with, had begun to shrink. Even those that kept in touch saw her with diminishing frequency. Recent events had made them uncomfortable around her.

Her therapist was more understanding, but Elizabeth left sessions feeling exhausted just as often as she felt refreshed. She didn't want to talk about her emotions, her guilt about Isaac's disappearance, their problems, her lack of sleep, her concern about Isaac's current whereabouts and well-being, the shock of his abandonment, her burdensome sadness, her even more burdensome *emptiness*... Sometimes she felt so drained that she wondered if it was even worth it to continue. Which was exactly the sort of thing she wasn't *supposed* to be wondering, the kind of thing that would worry all of *them* if they knew.

She yearned for more constant, less demanding company.

In these moments she missed Baby even more than she missed Isaac. After all, hadn't Isaac *chosen* to abandon her, leaving that nonsensical, melodramatic note in the mailbox? She still had that note, by itself, in a manila envelope in a box under her bed. At least Baby's disappearance had almost certainly been involuntary. She'd gotten lost in the woods, or been—

What? Taken? By whom? Or...what?

She didn't like to dwell on that. What mattered was that the little dog was gone and the chances of her still being alive—let alone returning to Elizabeth—might as well be nonexistent.

All of this was why, after three weeks of thorough consideration and planning, she stood in the Baraigne County Humane Society, looking down at a nine-year-old black Labrador mix named Bart.

"Black Bart," she said, affecting her best Val Kilmer-in-*Tombstone* drawl. "I'm here to spring you from this here joint."

Bart was a bit overweight, with enough gray around his snout to make him look even older than he was. Someone had tied a red bandana around his neck and he beamed up at her with a dog's equivalent of a wise smile. She'd already visited him twice before, but this time it was for keeps. She wondered if he knew it yet.

One of Bart's eyes was a little cloudy with a developing cataract. It reminded her of something she'd seen in her dreams; a white oval mask, at the top of a tall, cloaked form. She had first dreamt of it in her early teens, somewhere amidst that storm of self-discovery and the initial sink into depression. It had visited her only a few times since, but she had never quite forgotten it. At the castle, between Isaac's leaving and her own moving out, she'd even fancied she'd seen that same oval gleaming down at her from the foot of the bed.

Of course, it had just been the gibbous moon, shining in through the window.

What else could it have been?

She didn't like to dwell on that either.

Putting it out of her mind, she signed the adoption contract and paid the fee, which covered vaccines and a microchip.

"Would you like to register Bart's chip with your name and contact information?" the female attendant asked, ringing up Elizabeth's debit card. They were about the same age. "It's an additional ten dollars."

"Oh. Yes," Elizabeth said. "Yes, I definitely want to do that."

Once the fees were paid, the attendant opened Bart's kennel.

"Come on out, buddy." Elizabeth held up the little stuffed *Triceratops* she'd bought on the way over.

The old dog wagged his tail and took a few tentative steps out.

"That's a good boy."

Elizabeth had brought her own collar and leash—the collar was new, but the leash was one of Baby's old ones, made of faux brown leather. It was a little short for Bart, but it would do for now. She hooked him up and led him outside to her car, tossing the *Triceratops* in back. The June sun was bright and hot.

Bart needed a little help getting in on the passenger's side, but showed none of the nervousness to which Elizabeth had grown accustomed with Baby.

What was it her mom had told her? *The best way to get over losing a dog is to get a dog.* Elizabeth thought that might just be true. Wherever Isaac was, in Texas or somewhere else, she didn't need him anymore. Of course, knowing that didn't make missing him much easier, but it was enough to reassure her that she wasn't going to give up and die. She could go on.

"I can and I will," she said aloud as she pulled out of the parking lot. "I am. Right, Bart?"

Bart panted softly back at her from the passenger's seat, his pink tongue lolling from gray jaws, his clear eye bright and brown. He appeared to be smiling.

story notes

"Can't Stop Here": This story is the oldest in this collection, written during my sophomore year of college. The woman I was dating at the time lived in a tiny village about an hour away from me, and since we both still lived with fairly conservative parents, staying over at either house was awkward. Hanging out until midnight and then driving home seemed preferable most evenings, even though I often imagined monsters living in the dark just beyond my headlights. This story is the result of those imaginings, typed sitting up in bed sometime after 1 a.m. This is its first appearance.

"The 800-Pound Gorilla in the Room": I dreamt this story beginning-to-end in black-and-white, bookended by Rod Serling narration. I woke up and transcribed as much as I could remember into my phone, and later that day sat down to write. The story was done in a couple of hours, the fastest turnaround I've ever had from initial idea to finished draft. I think it's my best work so far. It first appeared in the *Saturday Evening Post* in 2019.

"From the Dusty Mesa": I wrote this one for the CLASH Books anthology *Walk Hand in Hand into Extinction: Stories Inspired by* True Detective. The open call came shortly after the end of *True Detective*'s first season, and sought stories exploring the show's existential themes and noir/horror mood. I was already a fan of the show, and thought of this as my chance to write a King in Yellow story by way of Laird Barron. After *Walk Hand in Hand into Extinction*, it was reprinted in the anthologies *Haunted are These Houses* (Unnerving, 2018) and *Nightmares in Yellow* (Oxygen Man Books, 2021).

"The Duelists": When I was twelve, I joined the then-new Point Fencing Club in Champaign, Illinois. At fourteen, I quit the sport and read *The*

Lurking Fear and Other Stories, my first direct exposure to the works of H. P. Lovecraft (the 1982 Del Rey paperback edition; I still remember that bloodcurdling Michael Whelan cover art!). At twenty-two, I decided to put these influences together. This one first appeared (with the British spelling "The Duellists") in *Swords Against Cthulhu* (Rogue Planet Press, 2015) and was reprinted in a limited chapbook of my earliest Lovecraftian stories, *Nods to the Master* (Unnerving, 2018).

"The Vindication of Y'ha-nthlei": There was this idea I couldn't shake about Lovecraft's Deep Ones rising up in vengeance after the events of *The Shadow Over Innsmouth* and engaging in protracted open war with the surface world. I wrote five or six stories chronicling this war, from the Deep Ones' first retaliatory strikes in the 1930s to an alternate twenty-first century in which mankind barely survives under amphibian rule. Only two of these ended up being any good at all: this one, which first appeared in *Whispers from the Abyss, Vol. 2: The Horrors That Are & Shall Be* (01 Publishing, 2015)…

"In Their Reeking Talons": …and this one, which appears here for the first time. The H. P. Lovecraft Historical Society's release of the *Dagon: War of Worlds* audio drama in 2015 contributed to my decision to move on from the "Deep Ones' revenge" idea, which I admit wasn't the most original concept even then. But I'm also a big sucker for 1950s monster movies, and I think this story is as much a tribute to films like *The Blob* as it is to anything Lovecraft wrote. I also wanted to write a story about the disillusion (and dissolution) of a closet cultist.

"She Said She Was a Magic Mama": Another story featuring mind-altering tentacles. This began as a superficially Lovecraftian riff on Kafka: a man wakes up to find his hand has been replaced by a tentacle. The first draft ended on the reveal that the man's conservative wife—and not his drug-dispensing mistress—was responsible for the transformation, but I decided to take it further. Nobody gets out of this one unscathed, except, perhaps, for the corrupt police captain (an unfortunately all-too realistic outcome). This is one of my nastier stories, and first appeared, perhaps appropriately, in *Trigger Warning: Short Fiction with Pictures* in 2019.

"The Worst": A road trip is more fun with a partner. In 2015 I entered a Lovecraftian short story contest in the *Providence Journal*. I submitted my best pastiche at the time, called "The Terrible Grimoire," and placed in the top 13 of some 200 entries, winning an invitation to read at a welcoming party for NecronomiCon Providence. My partner and I got some last-minute time off and made the trip in much the same way it's described here, *sans* (as far as I know) any invisible monsters. This story first appeared in *Unnerving Magazine* #5 in 2018.

"Hairworm": This story was inspired by a video I saw online of a parasitic horsehair worm emerging from the abdomen of its live praying mantis host. It horrified me, as did learning that certain species of these worms can infect a host insect's brain, causing it to seek water and drown itself—thus allowing the adult worm to escape and reproduce. It got the wheels turning, and I tried to write about a *Body Snatchers*-style alien invasion as an exploration of masculine loneliness.

"A Gator We Should Turn to Be": In 2017 I had an idea for a recurring character: a hardboiled, rock-loving career criminal known as the Midnight Witch. She gets into trouble all across America throughout the late 1960s and '70s, always escaping violent ends by the skin of her teeth and the skill of her aim. As of this writing I've completed seven very loosely connected stories featuring her, and sold three of them. This was the second, included here because it leans far more into horror than the rest. It first appeared in the *Norwegian American* in 2018, with a beautiful accompanying illustration by Inkshark.

"Like Nothing You've Ever Seen Before!": I wrote this one as a fake film essay, the kind you'd find printed with a special-edition release of some obscure cult film (something along the lines of the Criterion Collection or, maybe more appropriately, Vinegar Syndrome). I'd wanted to write a story about the making of a lost monster movie for a while, and ultimately landed on this method of telling it after several false starts. Just as "In Their Reeking Talons" is my Lovecraftian tribute to *The Blob*, this is my scaled-down, exploitation-infused homage to something like *Gorgo*. It appears here for the first time.

"Anatomy of a Broiler Oven": This is my pizza story. If you're a follower of the small-press horror world, you've probably already guessed that this was written for an anthology called *Tales from the Crust*. The challenge the editors put forth was to write a serious horror story about pizza. I recalled burning my hands one night making dinner while tipsy, combined that with the old bereavement and self-destructive bitterness of a college breakup, and the story rose from there. It didn't make the cut for the anthology, but I still enjoy it quite a bit. This is its first appearance anywhere.

"He Who Takes from Gwangi": I will always love dinosaurs. Some of the first stories I ever wrote were violent vignettes about prehistoric life, but for years I was hesitant to attempt a serious dinosaur story. The legacy of *Jurassic Park* weighed on me, along with every time travel and lost continent story ever written. Finally, I decided to just go for it, realizing that a vague supernatural explanation for the dinosaurs' presence was better (for my purposes, anyway) than getting bogged down in the complexities of genetic engineering, quantum physics, or environmental geography. The story appears here for the first time.

"In Kansas": Another aquatic monster story, and a prehistoric one. I used to work in an office building much like the one described here, and every spring the parking lot flooded. Once it got so bad that water was coming in under the doors on the ground level, and we were all effectively stranded there for a couple of hours after work. That's the genesis of this story. I asked myself what could be worse than being stranded in an office building surrounded by mosasaur-infested waters, and then tried to answer that question. This story appears here for the first time.

Nightbird: This one has been discussed in a handful of podcasts and blog interviews, but something they don't get much into is that this story is semi-autobiographical. I really did grow up in a castle in Central Illinois, I worked at a Christian bookstore, and I lost my virginity at sixteen to a self-proclaimed witch in a Victorian farmhouse (she was *not* two thousand years older than me). Some complexities ensued that didn't make it into the novella, though most were magnified, twisted, or wholly invented. I later fell in love with someone who suffered from extreme depression, and in the worst moments of our relationship I found myself preoccupied with the comforts and excitements of the past. *Nightbird* was originally published by Unnerving in 2018 as a standalone paperback.

acknowledgments

FOR SETTING ME on the paths that led to some of these stories, thanks to Bruce Busboom, Marcia Busboom, Michael Vitoux, Elizabeth Mueller, Phoenyx Nova, Sarah Snodgrass, Seth Mowrer, Bill Van Siclen, Alan Rosenberg, Janaya Kizzie, Brent Endsley, Brian Sullivan, David James Keaton, and Max Booth III.

For helping me believe in these stories, thanks to Shelby Koehne, Brittany Busboom-Miller, Seth Hubbell, Charles Schroeder, Nathan Carson, William Tea, Hannah Green, Jill Monroe, Danger Slater, Adrian Shotbolt, Erica Ruppert, Michael Sieber, Renee Miller, Lisa Quigley, Mackenzie Kiera, Leo X. Robertson, Sara Tantlinger, Morgan K. Tanner, Thomas Joyce, Lenore Sagaskie, David W. Barbee, Michael Wehunt, Matt Brandenburg, Sam Richard, Thomas Trumpinski, Jaffa Kintigh, Crista Carmen, and Mona LeSueur.

For taking chances on these stories, thanks to Gavin Chappell, Kat Rocha, Cristoph Paul, Leza Cantoral, Jason J. Marchi, Kat Rocha, Eddie Generous, Erin Sweet Al-Mehairi, Emily C. Skaftun, Andy Hollandbeck, Eric Lindbom, Duane Pecise, and, of course, Scarlett R. Algee.

Additional thanks to S. L. Edwards, Scott R. Jones, Sean Leonard, Don Noble, K. Allen Wood, John Boden, Mercedes Yardley, Laird Barron, Andrew and Miranda Cork, and the shades of William Peter Blatty, Ray Bradbury, Robert W. Chambers, Ray Harryhausen, Jimi Hendrix, H. P. Lovecraft, Millicent Patrick, George C. Scott, Rod Serling, Irvin Yeaworth, Frank Zappa, and Warren Zevon.

about the author

(Photo by Alisa Nicholle)

DAVID BUSBOOM is a science editor and lifelong Illinoisan who enjoys black coffee, heavy music, and dark fiction. His writing has appeared in *Shock Totem*, *Unnerving Magazine*, the *Saturday Evening Post*, *MYTHIC*, and *Planet Scumm*, among others. *Every Crawling, Putrid Thing* is his debut collection. Find him online at davidbusboom.com or on Facebook or Twitter (@DavidBusboom).

CPSIA information can be obtained
at www.ICGtesting.com
Printed in the USA
LVHW020457300822
727158LV00003B/165